THE THING ABOUT DAD

Pete Fanning

Immortal Works LLC
1505 Glenrose Drive
Salt Lake City, Utah 84104
Tel: (385) 202-0116

Cover Art by Ashley Literski
http://strangedevotion.wixsite.com/strangedesigns

This book is a work of fiction. Names, characters, businesses, organizations, places, events and incidents either are the product of the author's imagination or are used fictitiously. Any resemblance to actual persons, living or dead, events, or locales is entirely coincidental.

ISBN 978-1-953491-29-9 (Paperback)
ASIN B09N38Q22Z (Kindle)

For Dad

CHAPTER 1

Somewhere in Virginia our two-day, five-state journey came to a weary stop in the driveway of a strange house. I looked through a smear of mangled wings and bug guts on the windshield, to a weeping willow tree sagging in the heat. Its wilted leaves seemed to be begging for a breeze.

"Well?" Dad said, waiting for my reaction as the car ticked and hissed. My gaze followed the brick walkway to the porch where the ferns spilled from hanging baskets, as though searching for water between the large white columns.

"This is it?" I asked, a glint of hope catching my voice.

Hot as it was, I had to admit, the house was cool. Dad called it a bungalow, but to me, with its big green shutters and the upstairs window jutting right out onto the roof, it looked like a big clubhouse.

Dad threw his hands up. "This is it."

Untangling my feet from the nest of candy wrappers, potato chip bags, and soda bottles, I crawled out of the car, shaking my legs to life as we climbed the steps. Dad watched me closely, still trying to sell me on this little adventure, like he had been since the day he came home and announced his big promotion. Wasn't happening. There was nothing he could say to make me like Virginia. I was thirteen and would have to start over at some random middle school, having ditched my old friends and abandoned my spot as co-captain of the hockey team. He was the parent and I was the hostage.

Promotion. More like a *demotion*. Like I wanted to be here, choking down thick, muggy air in mid-July on the porch of some strange house—even if it did have a porch swing I was dying to test out.

Dad hung an arm around my shoulder. *Here comes the sales pitch,* I thought. "Look, I'm nervous too. I've lived in North Country my whole life, just like you. But sometimes life hurls opportunities at us, and we have to take chances."

I glanced up to my captor, his stormy blue eyes upbeat and hopeful. He was good with the pep talks, I'd give him that. Otherwise I wouldn't have gotten in the car. I'd still be in Grandpa's house, sipping a frosty Coke and watching the Rangers' game on his old floor model television. I dropped my eyes, not wanting to have the same tired conversation again.

Dad took the hint, sliding his arm off me and then slapping the beam above our heads with a stretch. "The movers should be here soon," he said with a nudge. "Come on, I'll give you a quick tour."

The house was stifling hot. Dad scampered to the living room and adjusted the thermostat, and the vents rattled to life.

"Please tell me that's air conditioning," I said, running my hand along the stone fireplace. I'd never lived in a house with air conditioning. Never needed to until now.

The sun streamed through two small windows on either side of the fireplace, bouncing off the polished floors. It smelled like new paint on the walls. Again, the place was sweet, but I was holding out because I hadn't seen my room yet.

An archway led to the kitchen, then out to a large wooden deck facing a wall of trees. "Okay," Dad said, rubbing his hands together dramatically. "Time for the moment of truth."

I followed him up the stairs where, even if the house was actually on fire it couldn't have been much hotter. Dad motioned to the rooms. "You're on the right, I'm on the left. The bathroom is straight ahead."

I hung a right and opened the door, wiping sweat from my forehead. Wow, okay. My room was huge, way bigger than home. More new smells encircled me, of cedar and floor polish. The ceilings sloped downwards to the large window overlooking the neighborhood. I looked out to the street where a kid putted around the curb on his bike. When he glanced up I eased back.

Dad's room was even bigger than mine, and he had his own door to the bathroom. The perks of paying rent, I guessed. Bending down, I held my face over the vents to make sure cool air was blowing. Dad chuckled. "It works, Jack."

"Just testing," I said, standing and relishing the icy blast up my shorts. "So how do you think Grandpa's doing?"

"I'm sure he's fine. Probably enjoying the peace and quiet without you banging on the drums," he said with a smile. Dad had jokes.

We'd checked in with Papa last night from the hotel, but still, it was hard leaving him back in upstate New York. It had always been just the three of us, and I liked it that way. Where Dad was laid back, Grandpa was tough as rust. He'd fought in Vietnam and had all sorts of medals and pictures and even his uniform. But Grandpa wasn't *all* tough guy, he could be cool—his jokes were epic. Dad said he'd softened up over the years, since Grandma passed. I wondered if the same thing happened to Dad after Mom died.

Some rumbling outside. The sneeze of air brakes. I ran for the window. "They're here!"

We rushed downstairs and out to the porch. The moving truck jerked and jostled as it hopped the curb, backing onto the grass and lurching for the steps. Dad jumped down and helped guide the truck in after the driver nearly took out a row of boxwoods. Finally, we waved him to a halt.

The doors creaked open and two of the oldest movers alive hobbled out of the truck. "How ya'll doing?" The driver croaked, wiping his brow with a bandanna. I snorted at his drawl. Dad cut his eyes my way. He'd said his company was paying for the move and these guys came with the deal.

When the back door slid up, it looked like the truck had rolled over twice and then flipped once more to be sure everything was overturned and collapsed. My stomach twisted, because my drum set—my most cherished possession in the world—was somewhere in the midst of the wreckage.

One of the movers, Harry or Larry (I could only make out the *arry*), whistled low and then muttered something I couldn't understand. Dad shrugged, and we began sorting through the mess.

Thankfully, most of the fallen boxes were Dad's books. Not sure why the geniuses set the books on top of everything, but then again I'm not a professional mover. We dug in, got my bed upstairs, then my desk—the bottom of which still had a few *Monsters Inc.* stickers stuck to it from forever ago. And finally, in the back, safe and sound and thankfully unblemished, we found my kit, the one thing I could not live without.

Out in the yard I inspected each piece for damage. Dad knelt beside me, wiping his brow with a towel. Everyone was soaked with sweat.

"How's it look? Everything okay?"

I nodded. "I think so."

"Nice. Hey, looks like we have company."

I looked up to find the kid I'd seen out the window shuffling over. He wore a hat that was way too big for his head, crooked glasses, and his stick legs sprouted out of loose socks and untied high-top sneakers.

"Is that a drum set?"

"Um, yeah," I said with a smirk, looking over my kick drum. The chrome of my snare drum sparkled in the bright sunshine.

"Cool," the kid said. He fixed his hat and sat down. I looked over to him and he smiled. "I'm Trevor Walker." His freckles bounced when he spoke.

"I'm Jack. Dufresne."

He hovered over me for a while, firing off question after question, clapping his hands in front of his face to bat away the swarms of gnats. *So, you play the drums? What grade are you in? Are ya'll moving in?*

"Yeah, me and my dad," I said to his last question with a laugh. He laughed too.

"Cool."

With my drums safe, I helped Dad haul in some chairs. Trevor, my new shadow, tagged along at my hip. But it was kind of nice to have some company after being stuck in the car for the past few days, and besides, listening to him babble gave me something to do other than grumble to Dad about the heat.

Late afternoon, Trevor's parents arrived to welcome us. Trevor's mom went through the introductions—Mr. Walker was a dentist, and she was a teacher. They lived at the bottom of the street and loved the neighborhood, blah blah blah, something about their daughter at a friend's house.

They seemed okay. They didn't stay long, dragging Trevor away and letting us get back to work after the movers dropped something in the other room. On their way out, Mrs. Walker offered dinner again, but Dad assured them we'd be fine—which meant we were ordering pizza.

After they left, we cranked up the tunes. My dad is forty but he plays guitar and likes to hang out. Sure, he can be strict and stern and all parental and stuff, but he's a kid at heart and pretty easy to read.

At some point I got stuck with taking junk down to the basement. At the bottom of the steps, I dropped a box of books and yanked on the overhead pull strings until I found a light that worked. The basement was unfinished, with cinderblock walls and pipes and wires running along the ceiling. In other words, it was the perfect spot to jam. Near the back, I found a storage room with some old dusty furniture and shelves filled with nuts and bolts that jingled when Harry or Larry stomped down the steps, piled some wrinkled boxes in the corner with a grunt, then marched back upstairs, shutting the door behind him and leaving me alone with the plodding footsteps and muffled voices over my head.

It was nice and cool down there, and one of those boxes contained the hockey cards Grandpa had given me just before we left. It was his *The Miracle on Ice* set and he'd said it was worth a little bit of money. Dad and I hadn't exactly labeled the boxes, so I just ripped into the one on top. Board games. Great. I moaned at the thought of the two of us sitting around playing Scrabble on a Saturday night, an ancient dictionary cracked open as we argued over my use of a slang.

I set the games aside and tore into box number two—a bunch of old spiral bound composition books like you'd get for school. Only there were maybe twenty of them. I ran my finger along the metal binds, then for some reason, picked one out.

On the first splotchy yellow page I saw my mom's name, *Ellie*, then my name. It was a journal or something. I swallowing a big, musty gulp of basement air and fell against the cool cinderblock wall, flipping through the pages, catching little bits and pieces.

I had a dream about you last night...

Flip.

Jack had his first recital at school...

Flip.

Life isn't the same without you...

I shut the book and clutched it to my chest. What in the world? Of all the stuff my dad and I talked about—music, sports, school—Ellie, my mom, was not on the list. I wouldn't even know where to begin. It was why what I was holding—written proof she had been a real person and not just some smile in a frame—felt like a long lost treasure map.

My heart galloped. I slid down to the floor, a shiver rippling through my skin as I flipped back to the first page.

Dear Ellie,

The upstairs door swung open and I scrambled to my feet, kicking over the pile of board games and sending dice and cards and Monopoly money across the floor. I fumbled my way back toward the boxes when Dad called down, "Jack?"

I stuffed the notebook back with the others, glanced at the mess on the floor, and then bounded up the stairs full stride.

Dad gave me a once over. "You okay?"

"Yeah, I'm okay," I said, a little out of breath and lightheaded from the stairs or the box or just, everything. I tried to meet his gaze but looked away, back toward the steps, unable to come up with anything to say. Thankfully, Tom Petty blared off the empty walls, his familiar voice making things almost normal again.

Dad patted me on the shoulder and said something about going to find the towels.

Life in Virginia was off to a very weird start.

CHAPTER 2

"Well, that was...interesting." Dad ran a finger over the doorjamb, gouged by Harry and Larry when they banged the couch through. I gulped down a Gatorade and watched the truck jerk then stall before lurching up the road.

Worse than hauling stuff, was the unpacking stuff. We unpacked picture frames, speakers, huge knots of tangled cords, remote controls, markers, and all other sorts of junk. We waded through the mess. We ordered pizza and listened to music. The cable company said it would be a week before they could come out. Not that it mattered, the TV was wrapped in a quilt, somewhere.

Boxes and end tables lined the walls. Shelves were scattered all over the place. Grandpa's old rolltop desk and chair still held a whiff of home.

Sure, the house was a wreck, but at least it had cooled down. We moved to the kitchen where Dad rummaged through the mess, looking for cups. "So when I go to work on Monday, are you going to be all right by yourself?"

"Yes, Dad, I'm not a baby."

"The Walkers seem nice. They said you could hang out at their place with uh, with um..."

"Trevor."

"Trevor. He seemed okay, didn't he?"

I shrugged. Dad wiped pizza sauce from his mouth. I dug in for a second slice as we looked over the wreckage. Dad with his beer, me with my soda. A roll of paper towels between us.

"Jack, I know you don't want to hear this again, but you're going to have to give this thing a chance."

I was about to remind him how our hockey team had made it to the finals last year when over his shoulder I saw our family picture already up on the mantel. It was the one in the driftwood frame, Mom and Dad's heads touching, a gust of wind tossing Mom's hair around as a wave broke in the background. Dad was grinning, holding me with one arm. I'm maybe a year and a half old and slathered in sunscreen.

Looking at the picture reminded me of the boxes in the basement. What was in there? What was he writing about Mom? About me?

Before I could think more about it, Dad hopped up and rinsed his plate at the sink. "Okay, tomorrow is Saturday. Let's get the living room straight, then get the dishes unpacked, and if there's time I'll show you the sights around town."

I broke off my thoughts about Mom. "Sights? Like what?

"Well, there's a lot of history around here."

"I want to get my drums set up. Can we jam tomorrow?"

He turned off the faucet and looked for something to dry his hands. I tossed the roll of paper towels. He caught it and grinned. "I'll have to find my guitar, but I think we can manage that."

I've played drums since I was seven, when Dad brought home a tiny toy drum set, with "The Muppets" on the kickdrum. Anyway, the "drums" were nothing more than paper, and so I destroyed the whole set in a week and cried until he got me a real set. He did, a sky-blue Pearl set he found on Craigslist. The one I had until two Christmases ago when I upgraded.

Music is our thing. My dad was in a band back in the day. The Four Casts. Like the weather, get it? I shouldn't have to tell you there were four guys in the band, although I'd been waiting in the wings if the drummer ever quit.

I stole another glance at Mom in the picture. I don't know why, but it felt like spiders were crawling down my neck. I couldn't stop thinking about what he'd written. Maybe because all I really knew about my mom was that she died when I was three. Hit by a tractor trailer on I-87. The rest I'd pieced together from Grandpa or Aunt Genna, Uncle Ronnie. To them she was the star of their memories, some clear, some vague, some changing depending on who was telling the story. But no matter who was telling it, every story of my mom ended with a faraway smile and a shake of the head. Except for me. I had no stories to tell. For me, she was like a ghost.

With half a pizza devoured we stepped out on the front porch. The evening air was still thick even as it was going on nine. A pink smolder held the horizon. Dad gave the porch swing a tug, testing the weight, and we both stared at the ceiling, waiting for it to come crashing down. When it didn't fall, he cautiously set his butt in the middle, and the swing squeaked a little but held. I took the wooden Adirondack chair, savoring its name as I listened to the thrum of the jungle critters coming from the woods.

Dad took a big, dramatic breath. "Nice out here, huh?"

I shrugged. What a dork.

The swing creaked in time with the crickets, as the streetlamp flickered to life down at the end of the street, right over the hoop. Out on the lawn lay a heap of boxes and tape from all the unpacking. At last, a slow breeze swept over us, fluttering the tentacles of the Willow tree.

Dad and I were in Virginia. Mom's face was in a picture frame. And maybe, just maybe, all the answers to my questions lay in a box in the basement.

CHAPTER 3

Hillridge. Yeah, okay, I get it now. Our street was on a hill. The next street was a hill. Downtown was one big hill. The town was like a roller coaster.

In Plattsburgh, everything was flat. I could ride my bike for miles, through the heart of town, out to Point Au Roche and back, without even getting winded. It was great. Wherever I needed to go, I hopped on my bike and arrived in ten minutes.

I set my head back. "I guess they don't cross-country ski around here, huh?"

Dad laughed. "No, I don't think so. But think about all of the sledding hills."

I rolled my eyes at the thought of skiing and sledding, as it was ninety-one degrees outside. And ninety-one degrees here was no ordinary ninety-one degrees. The smothering humidity hung like a weight on my back. So when Dad mentioned finding our swimming trunks and checking out the public pool at the park, I was ready. I wasn't sure what people did down here *besides* swim.

We climbed more hills, then zig-zagged our way through town looking for Baxter Park. I'd never seen so many churches, a steeple on every corner, sometimes two or three in a row. I navigated Dad's phone, and after a few wrong turns, we pulled up to the pool where every single parking space was taken.

The place was packed. Colorful noodles and floats, round tubes and hats—nothing but arms, heads, and legs from one end to the other. A body of water, all right. Dad and I sat in the car for a moment as the antagonizing screams and squeals and sounds of splashing water beckoned. I looked at him and he shrugged. We grabbed our towels and headed for the water.

Entering, I hustled to an open section of lounge chairs. The deep end of the pool with the diving boards looked to be the only place to get in. Dad tossed his towel on the chair and motioned at the high dive. "I think you should start off strong."

I cupped my hands to my eyes to shield the glare bouncing off the water, squinting toward the lower diving board where a line stood. Then I looked up, way up, to the highest high dive I'd ever seen. It was so high it needed flashing red lights so planes could steer clear.

Dad grinned. "You really going off that thing?"

"Uh, maybe. You?"

"No, I don't think so," Dad said, his sunglasses aimed upwards to the sky. I'm not sure why, but it felt like I needed to prove something. I looked at him, then over to the board.

"I'm doing it."

"You sure?" Dad said, breaking out the SPF60.

I shrugged. "Why not?"

I sucked it up and tore off my shirt, my Plattsburgh pale on full display as I marched to the diving board. My feet smacked the hot puddles on the concrete, and I squinted as the sun blinded me with its glare. The kids waiting to go off the regular board grew quiet as I approached Mt. Everest. From her perch above the pool, the lifeguard whistled, and I froze. "Jaylen, I've already told you three times, no running!"

The running kid—Jaylen— came to a dripping stop behind me, huffing and puffing as a puddle formed at his feet. "Sorry, Lisa," he called to her, twisting on one of the braids of his starter dreadlocks. He smirked at me then glanced at the smaller board.

"You diving?"

"I uh," I looked up, and up. Jaylen's eyes went big as he followed my gaze.

"Oh. You're going off the high dive?" He turned and called over to a kid ahead of me. "Yo, Sean, this dude is going up the high dive!"

Every face turned. Then it was like a swarm, and I was in the middle of a sopping wet huddle, with nowhere to go but up.

"The last person to jump off the high dive was Tevin James, and he hasn't been back to the pool in weeks," Jaylen said with a devilish smile. Even Lisa, the lifeguard, had swiveled in her chair to watch. "Just be sure to tuck in," Jaylen said, crouching. "T belly flopped something bad. Could hear him crying underwater."

"Oh, that's...um..." With that in mind, I started up the ladder, more to escape the horror stories than jump off the board. The steps clanged as my feet climbed higher and higher, and then I was on the plank. I made the mistake of looking down, only to find the kids below watching intently to see if I'd go through with jumping off. Great. I'd been in Virginia one night, and I was already in a jam.

Dad waved to me from across the sea of floaties and beach balls and bobbing heads in the water. He made a tucking motion like a doofus and I blushed. *Got it, Dad.* I nodded, seeing how everyone in and out of the crowded pool, including the lifeguards, had gone silent.

My legs wobbled as I set my feet on the diving board. I may as well have been up on the Empire State Building. I held tight to the railing, took a deep breath, and forced my eyes to stay open. The last thing I wanted to do was go flailing over the side. I took a timid first step, my feet feeling the gritty surface of the board for grip. *Well, here goes.* I let go of the railing, took four steps, and found myself at the end of the road. I made the mistake of looking down, waaaaay down. Jaylen cheered from below.

The next thing I knew I was hurdling through the air like a skydiver. My hair left my head as the wind attacked my face. My freefall seemed to last forever, giving me plenty of time to say a prayer. I tried to tuck. To ball up. To do anything but what must have looked like jumping jacks. Then, *splash*.

My feet hit first as I reached the water in a Jack knife/Mummy/please-don't-let-me-die hybrid flop. I plunged to the bottom, flailing and wiggling to be sure everything still worked. It did. I shot off the floor of the pool and broke through the water to sunshine, gasping for breath.

"Dude! That was amazing!" Jaylen called from the ledge. Lisa stood in her chair, glaring at him for running again. I smiled as the other kids pointed to the still wobbling diving board with wide eyes and laughter, until another kid summoned the courage to climb the ladder. Dad, in the shallow end, pumped his fist. I ducked back underwater.

Jaylen introduced me to Sean and Freddie, and we took turns diving on the normal diving board, playing a game they called "Leisure Diving" where we'd spring off and pose in midair like we were sleeping or talking on the phone just before we'd hit the water. It was a good time, and it was cool hanging out with people who weren't my dad. For the first time in a while I didn't worry about being in a strange place or starting completely over at a new school next month.

CHAPTER 4

The box was gone.

I'd snuck down to the basement while Dad was hanging the shower curtain. Sure enough, the board games had been cleaned up, and the other boxes were stacked neatly against the wall. No sign of *the* box. I looked in the back, under the stairs, but only found our sun faded cooler, our skis, and the snowboards we'd never use again. Only Dad's tools back in the workshop.

I was kind of bummed, then again Dad would have to go to work eventually, when I planned on a more thorough search.

Meanwhile, the basement was nice and cool and maybe a bit musty but it would work just fine for Dad and me I finished getting everything set up, trying to get it just like it had been back home, even the posters in the same order. Thing was, it wasn't home. No wood stove. No Grandpa upstairs. No friends next door and no hockey games down at the pond.

I hung some posters and found my sticks and called upstairs. Dad's size thirteens thumped overhead. The door opened. "Yeah?"

"Wanna jam?"

"You know it."

I adjusted my high hat. Dad came shuffling down and looked around, smiling in approval at how I'd already hooked everything up. He strapped on his guitar and fiddled with the amp. The familiar crackle and static buzzed between us. After some tuning up we got down to business.

Dad turned to me with a grin as he cranked out the first few cords to "Wild Thing." I crashed a cymbal and we found our rhythm.

"Wild Thing" isn't rocket science to play, and we kept it simple. I knew what I was doing, but I was no John Bonham or anything (the drummer for Led Zeppelin). Dad had to duck his head occasionally not to hit the bulb hanging from the ceiling. I laughed as he kicked and shuffled around, finding his groove. He always cracked me up with his faces when he played, especially when he started swinging the guitar around like a machine gun. I missed a beat, but he just went with it.

"Wild Thing" morphed into a little jam we'd come up with over the years. An Allman Brothers-like riff where I could wing it on the drums. I put a little something extra on the beat, and Dad played loud as all our worry of the past few days began to melt away while we broke in the basement.

We rolled into a lackluster version of "Smoke on the Water" before falling apart. We joked about the neighbors calling the cops. But it was early still, just after eight.

"You hungry?" Dad asked. "I picked up propane for the grill."

I wiped my forehead and nodded. I could always eat. Dad said he thought so, and we climbed the old wooden stairs to the kitchen where he already had two steaks marinating in a bowl. Back home we always grilled on Saturday nights. Sometimes the guys would come over for band practice and afterwards we'd have a feast. Grandpa would fiddle with his hearing aids and complain about the noise, but he never had any problems with the food.

With the grill fired up, Dad slapped on the two steaks with two potato packets. The grill sizzled and I breathed it in, gazing into the solid darkness of the woods behind the house.

"Sure is peaceful," Dad sighed. I silently agreed. The steaks tinged the evening air with a savory aroma, and soon we were talking music.

We ate outside. Dad laughed about my high dive antics, doing his own impression of my face that had me cracking up.

"Yeah, but at least I jumped off."

"So, that Jaylen kid, he's around your age?"

I slapped at the mosquitoes feasting on my legs. "Dad. I know how to make friends."

"I know you do."

We let the crickets do the talking—a pulsing in the dark that Dad called katydids and locusts and whatever else was lurking in the shadows. The heat was only beginning to let go of the evening, and it was almost comfortable with the sun below the trees.

Dad sat back and set his arms behind his head, revealing two perfectly matching pit stains. It seemed all we did was sweat around here. "So, I go to work on Monday. Are you going to be okay?"

"Yeah, I want to explore the woods. And hook up the PlayStation." *Oh, and find your journals. I really want to do that.*

"Okay, the Walkers said you were more than welcome to hang out there."

"I'll be fine, Dad."

Virginia. How in the world had this happened? Well, I guess I knew how it happened. I remembered the exact day—April 5th. Dad came home and asked if we could talk. *A talk* is never a good thing. Like how we'd *talked* after I got into a fight at the park, or when we *talked* after I hit the city plow with a snowball. *Talks* usually began with a deep sigh and ended with me getting grounded.

So when Dad said we were moving I thought he was kidding. I mean, I'd spent my whole life in Plattsburgh. All my family was nearby in Montreal and Vermont, some cousins in

Boston. I'd been to Florida once on vacation but we'd flown. Stepping off the plane in Florida didn't really count because one, I knew I was going home, and two, did I mention I knew I was going home? This was different. My dad was serious.

I said no way. I could stay with Grandpa. Papa wouldn't mind, we'd moved in with him when I was in the fifth grade, right after Nana had been diagnosed with cancer. I guess things had been rough for both Papa and Dad. And I always thought the three of us living together made sense.

But wouldn't you know it, even Grandpa left me hanging. He said I had to at least give it a shot. *Gee thanks, Grandpa, good to know you have my back.* So I told them I'd rather go to an orphanage. Drastic, I know, but it had the desired effect. And as bad as I felt for saying it, I was too mad to apologize. Besides, no one had asked me how I felt about moving. I wanted to ask if we'd be moving if Mom was around. But I couldn't.

Over the next few weeks I tried to forget about it. Even as June sat looming on the calendar like a bullseye. May flew right by. Boxes arrived at the house. Dad packed and I moped. I never packed. I made wisecracks about the south. And the whole time, even with all my threats, I knew I wasn't really going to stay. Because what would I do without my dad?

But if nothing else, I'm stubborn. And on the way down my dad finally cracked. He said if I gave it a try—a real shot—and I still didn't like it, we could move back. I jumped all over it, at least until he said I had to give it a year.

So that left us here, somewhere in the heart of Virginia, sweating on the deck and smacking mosquitoes off our legs.

"It's probably sixty degrees back home," I stated, just to rub it in.

Dad nodded, took a swig of his beer, and pointed to the sunset. "Yeah, but look at that." The sky gleamed, glowing pink and orange, smoldering behind the woods. It was impressive, but

I wasn't in the mood for conceding. I smacked my leg dramatically.

"I hope I don't catch malaria."

Dad nearly spit out his beer. Wiping his mouth, he leaned back and banged on the deck railing and...then I laughed too. Soon we were joking and cracking up just like old times. Our whoops and laughter bouncing off the house, swallowed up by holes of darkness in the woods.

Sure I wasn't happy about any of this, but at least we were together.

CHAPTER 5

Downstairs, Dad's spoon clinked against his bowl. I rubbed my eyes and for five or ten seconds I had no idea where I was. Another clank of the spoon and it hit me. I was on my bed, in my room. In Virginia.

I searched through the boxes until I found a pair of shorts and my long lost New York Rangers tee. In the kitchen Dad was at his laptop, sure enough, with a bowl of oatmeal under his chin. He looked up and offered his trademark greeting.

"There he is!"

He was entirely too chipper for my groggy brain. "Hey."

"So I may come home for lunch. The office is only four miles away, can you believe that?"

I shrugged. Wrong move. Dad sat back and took me in, his face going soft. I already knew what was coming. "So are you okay with this? I hate leaving you all alone."

"Yeah, Dad, I'm fine."

"Okay, well Mrs. Walker has the number," he said, getting to his feet, searching for his keys.

He rinsed his bowl and coffee mug, his face going soft again.

"I'm fine," I mumbled.

After more suggestions and questions, I practically had to push him out the door. Once he was gone I went for the Apple Jacks, but the fluttering in my chest quickly spread into a five-alarm fire. No sense in waiting to look for those journals. I slid my bowl away, ready to tear the house upside down.

I figured I'd start in the basement and work my way up. It

had to be here somewhere. I started down the steps. I just needed—

A few knocks at the door. It was 8:30 am.

I stopped, turned, then raced back up the stairs. Dad must have forgotten something. Whew, that was close.

I yanked the door open to find Trevor, the neighbor kid, with a seriously pretty girl standing behind him. A girl around my age.

"Hey Jack."

"Uh," my voice caught. I coughed. "Uh, hey."

He threw his hand back to the girl. "This is my sister, Miranda."

"Hi." Miranda stepped forward with a bounce. She was tall, with endlessly long legs. With one hand she held her hair up in a ponytail. Her eyes were light brown, or amber, or gold maybe. I couldn't decide because I had to force myself to stop staring.

"You okay?" Trevor asked with a snort.

"Oh, um yeah, sure. Hi," I said to Miranda, whose smile widened. Trevor scooted past me, and I opened the door wide to let them in, wishing I'd brushed my hair. Trevor's head swiveled to take in the room, his eyes gazing around. "Wow, you guys don't have much stuff. The Sanders had this place packed to the gills."

Miranda slapped Trevor on the arm, and he jerked it away. "What? I didn't mean it in a bad way," he said. I ran a hand through my hair, stealing a glance at my reflection in the door. Trevor craned his neck up the stairs.

"So where'd you put those drums?" he asked, shooting a look at his sister. She rolled her eyes and let her hair fall to her shoulders.

"In the basement. Why, you want to see them?"

"Yes!" he said, his excitement turning into a coughing fit. I snuck a glance at Miranda, who patted his back.

"Asthma," she said to me just as Trevor popped up, smiling and red. We shuffled down to the basement, Trevor wheezing behind me and Miranda casually following.

"Wow, they really cleaned this place up." I got the feeling Trevor knew something about every house on the street. "Whoa. You have a guitar, too?" He spun around. "Miranda!"

I pulled the string to the overhead light, Miranda's face lit up when she saw my dad's Fender. A quick glance my way, and she caught me staring. My heart did a drum roll. I laughed nervously and took a seat on my stool, picking up my sticks. Trevor bounced with excitement.

"Do you play?" I asked, nodding to the guitar.

Trevor turned to his sister. Miranda shrugged. "Not really. A little I guess."

Again, I had to make myself look away. It wasn't just that she was pretty, really pretty, she was also African American, while Trevor—redheaded and pale like his parents—was most certainly not. Was she adopted? It didn't matter, but it caught my attention.

"Play, Miranda." Trevor said. Miranda shot him a big sister glare. I smiled, tapping the foot pedal a couple of times as another bright smile spread across Miranda's face. At least until Trevor butted in again. "She sings too, don't you Miranda."

Miranda rolled her eyes. "Do you ever shut up, Trevor?"

I smiled and tapped out a soft beat. *Boom Clack, Boom Boom, Clack.*

"Is this yours, too?" Miranda asked, still eyeing Dad's Fender. Her voice was nice. Deep yet smooth and confident.

"No, it's my dad's," I said, feeling lamer by the second.

Trevor spun around. "You play with your dad? That's so cool."

"What does your mom play, the organ?" Miranda joked, looking around.

I stopped my tapping. I figured we might as well get this over with. "No, my mom's dead."

Her eyes went wide. "Oh gosh. I'm so sorry." She set her hand to her heart. I hit the foot pedal. *Boom, boom, boom, boom.*

I hopped up and turned on the amp. "So, does anyone want to play guitar?"

Trevor shoved Miranda toward me. I held out Dad's guitar. He'd kill me if he knew, but all the mom-talk made the risk worth taking. Miranda ducked under the strap. I handed her a pick.

She looked over the guitar and laughed. "I've never played an electric guitar before."

I shrugged with a grin. "It's the same idea. Just louder."

She strummed a couple of cords, carefully positioning her fingers on the frets. Clumsy at first but after a few tries she found her place, and I hopped back behind my drums. We fumbled to find a rhythm. Trevor offered to run home and grab his trumpet, but I motioned with a drumstick to the tambourine on the shelf.

Stopping and starting, we plowed along, laughing as we pieced together a song. That's the thing about playing music—or even just making noise—we could hang out and I didn't have to come up with something to say. At least until Miranda missed a chord and stomped her foot playfully.

"You're pretty good," I managed.

"Thanks, it's a little different."

Trevor jingled the tambourine. "Man, we rock!"

Boom. Boom.

Trevor giggled and jingled and we sat in our places, ears ringing, amp humming. After a few more "songs," we called it quits.

"Hey, you want to come over to our house?" Trevor asked. I glanced to Miranda, but she was locked into her phone.

I shrugged. "Sure."

Outside, the heat was gearing up for another day of torture. Trevor skipped ahead of us as we approached the end of the street. "My mom is worried about you being all by yourself. She won't even let Miranda stay by herself, and she's almost fourteen."

"Yes she does, dork," Miranda said rolling her eyes.

The Walkers' driveway was a curving, two-track gravel path beneath a tunnel of arching cherry trees. Thick, knotted vines threaded through the branches, lining the shade before latching onto the split rail fencing buried in a thicket of boxwoods, honeysuckle, and briars.

The tunnel opened to a field, leading to an A-frame type house, its windows gleaming in the sun. It was like walking onto a movie set.

Cue the dog. Under one of the willows, a dark mass scrambled to its feet, barking as he lumbered our way.

Trevor called out, "Wally!"

"He's uh, friendly right?" I tried to keep my voice from breaking.

Miranda looked at me like I was crazy. "Wally? No way. *Super* aggressive. Prepare to be mauled."

I laughed, but the dog was big enough to ride like a bull. He bypassed Miranda and Trevor, tail swishing, tongue waving, and slobber flying as he snorted to a stop at my feet. It was clear he was a lover not a fighter.

"He just wants to check you out," Trevor said. Wally gave me a once over, sniffing my legs and hands. I breathed a sigh of relief.

"He likes you." Miranda smiled.

Entering into the kitchen through the back door, my heart sank as Miranda scampered off, leaving me alone with her little brother. Trevor wasn't so bad, I guess. Besides, I didn't exactly have big plans for the day.

We found Mrs. Walker in the dining room, and Trevor launched into a play by play of our "jam session."

When we'd met earlier, Mrs. Walker had mentioned she taught English at Hillridge High. Now I watched as she swept up some folders from the table and offered me a seat. On the counter I cringed at the posters showing the stages of gingivitis. I thought about Wally.

"Please excuse the mess. We're always getting promotions in the mail."

"Makes me want to brush my teeth," I said, looking over all the pamphlets of browning teeth.

"Do you need a toothbrush?" Trevor asked, yanking one from a box. "My dad's a dentist, ya know."

"Oh, uh, sure," I said. It explained Miranda's smile. But what wasn't explained was how they were related. The thought vanished when Miranda returned and plopped down on the couch, phone in hand.

"Is Megan's mother picking you up?" Mrs. Walker asked, and Miranda nodded. Mrs. Walker turned to me, smiling politely.

"So Jackson, do you prefer to be called Jack?"

"Jack, or, either is fine." What a stupid answer, but I was caught trying to be cool and polite. I was neither. Miranda cut me a look and smiled. Mrs. Walker kept the questions coming.

"Are you going to Claremont Middle this year?"

"Yeah," I said, risking a glance at Miranda, still glued to her phone.

"Maybe Miranda can show you around?"

Miranda jerked her head to her mother. Trevor laughed. Luckily, before things got any more humiliating, a car pulled up outside.

"That's her. Bye mom. Bye dork. Nice to meet you, Jack or Jackson."

The door swung open before Miranda could escape. A girl stormed into the room. "Hi, Mrs. Walker," she said, flashing a metallic smile before she grabbed Miranda's hand. "Oh my gosh, Miranda, listen, so I went—"

She saw me and stopped midsentence. Miranda nodded my way. "Oh, this is Jack, maybe Jackson. He just moved in up the street. Jack, Megan. Megan, Jack. Come on let's go." Miranda pushed the girl out the door and they were gone, leaving me with Trevor and their mom.

"So, you want to see my room?" Trevor asked. I shrugged, looking back at the door.

So much for that.

CHAPTER
6

All week Trevor hung around my house. He was at the door every morning, alone, ready and waiting with questions. *What's New York like? Do you want to play the drums? Do you want to hear me play the trumpet? Do you want to shoot hoops? Ride bikes? Play with Wally?* I didn't mind it so much, but I did have a few questions of my own, not that I ever had a chance to ask them.

On Thursday I tagged along with Trevor and Miranda to the pool—a private pool that was far less crowded than Baxter Park. It was quiet and orderly and almost boring. I worked on my diving board skills while mostly everyone lay around talking. Miranda's friends whispered and giggled a whole lot, and Miranda was the only one who even bothered to get in the water. At least until Trevor started with the splashing.

Meanwhile Dad was full of surprises. First, he gave me his old iPhone. I'd been after him for one since last year and he'd never budged. But I guess dragging me down to Virginia then leaving me alone while he was at work had done the trick. Or maybe he figured we'd need to stay in touch. I was too busy messing with the phone to pay attention to the second surprise—that we were going to a baseball game with the Walkers. *All* of the Walkers, including Miranda.

The Hillridge Cardinals were a single A team, which meant they were light years away from the big time. Baseball was okay, but baseball in the south meant sitting on searing hot metal bleachers and sweating it out with rowdy fans screaming at the umpire in indecipherable grunts and whistles that would leave a UN translator scratching his head.

In the sixth inning, Miranda and I were sent to the concession stand for refills. Armed with a twenty from Dad, we climbed the steps, waiting in line where the wafts of popcorn and hotdogs pumping out of the snack bar hit my stomach with a bang. I was trying to think of something to say when Miranda swung around. "So, Megan thinks you're cute."

"Huh?" I said, then, catching up. "Oh, um, Megan? The one who's always giggling?"

"Yep, that's her." She laughed.

"Oh," I said again, as we moved up in line.

"Well don't get *too* excited," she said with a little grin. A sweaty guy wearing a sun visor waved us to the counter. "Anyway, she just wanted me to tell you, so...there, I've told you."

She spun around and stepped up to the counter. I followed, more interested in the messenger than the message.

I'd only had one sorta/kinda girlfriend back home. Sara Murphy. We'd gone to the Valentine's Day dance together back in February and I'd kissed her on the cheek. In the spring we sort of got sick of talking on the phone and just kind of stopped. My friends teased me all the time about having a girlfriend, so I can't say I was upset when things fizzled.

So yeah, I was no expert when it came to girls, and Miranda Walker was an advanced puzzle. Especially after we hung out most of the next week—with Trevor of course—hiking the paths in the woods behind their house. The Walkers even had a campsite beside the creek, where we kicked off our shoes and waded in the water, tossing rocks and laughing at Wally romping around.

It was cool, between hanging out and the game—at least until Friday, when her friends came over and she blew me off without a word, which left me with Trevor and his gazillion questions for the rest of the afternoon.

I made up an excuse to run home, figuring at least I had time to resume the journal hunt. I searched the basement again, just to be sure. Nothing. Then I tore through the small, insufferably hot storage nook in the attic. More nothing. I hit the closets, only to find cleaning supplies, winter coats, and hats. Blankets.

The only place left was Dad's room.

Dad never shut his door, so it didn't feel like I was doing anything wrong. I scanned under his bed, peeked in a few boxes of books near the window. Then I opened the closet. In the back corner, I found a box, a newer box, out of place amongst his shoes and sneakers.

Jackpot.

The notebooks near the back were scuffed and the pages were kind of torn. I plucked one right from the middle, telling myself maybe they were just budgets or boring insurance stuff even as I knew better. Sure enough, flipping through yellowed pages, there it was again: *Ellie*—written in the slant of his cursive that was kind of hard to read.

I swallowed hard, my chest tightening as I took a breath and opened to a random page, dated 3-14-16.

Jack had a hockey game today. I think he liked it. You should have seen him Ellie, gliding on the ice out there. He's gotten so big! I think he had fun too. After the game we had lunch with the rest of the team. Mostly moms, some dads. We enjoyed ice cream and had a good time. But sometimes the good times are the hardest. They leave me feeling cheated.

Later that night, as I tucked him in, he asked me not to die. He's eight. He's eight years old and asking me not to die. It was all I could do to rub his head and tell him everything would be okay...

Chills trailed down my arms, my breath ragged. This was so strange. I scanned the rippled page to the next paragraph, cocking my head to listen for Dad. The house was quiet. Only my own shaky breath as I read on.

3-28-16

Happy Birthday Ellie. The sun shined bright and golden today and I knew you were with us. It was nearly forty degrees out. We even went to the park! Jack's hair has gotten long and it curls like yours. He wants to cut it but I'm holding out on him. Yeah, call me selfish. Oh, and we read Charlotte's Web *tonight. I thought it would be weird, reading your favorite childhood book to our son, but it's not. Although I can't do it justice like you could. But he's enjoying it. We both are.*

I dropped the notebook to my lap. My dad wrote this? Mr. Upbeat and Positive? A little voice in my head demanded I set the notebook back into the box and slide the box into the closet and leave it all alone. But I couldn't. It existed now. I pulled out the first notebook, carefully; the front cover was worn and tearing away from the binder. I started on the first page, to read about my mom, about me, about the side of my dad kept hidden in a box.

7-29-12

Ellie, I can't begin to tell you how much I miss you. A part of me has been ripped away and I'm unfit to do this alone. I've kept some of your things, shirts and scarves that still have your smell to them. Or maybe I just imagine they do. Am I crazy? Greg thinks I need to let go. I can't do it. I have to do it, but I can't. How can I raise Jackson without you? That wasn't the plan. It's almost been a year and I think about you every minute. I can't go to sleep because you haunt my dreams. I look at our son and I see your eyes. You're inside of him. It's just too hard… If only—

My phone buzzed and I jumped like I'd been electrocuted. Dad's name on the screen as I let it ring, staring at the phone but too afraid to answer because he'd know. He'd hear it in my voice. I wiped my eyes, surprised to find they were moist. The phone went silent and I tossed it on the bed and closed the notebook. Carefully placing everything in the box, I set the lid back on top and pushed it to the back of the closet where I found it.

The phone chimed with a new voicemail. I drifted downstairs and fell on the couch, unable to get my dad's words out of my head. The room felt fake, like the set of a stage. Everything in there seemed meaningless. I stared at the ceiling fan making lazy rotations overhead and bit my lower lip. My eyes roamed to the books on the shelf. Some of them were Mom's. I jumped to my feet. It's why he was so crazy about those books. It was like all he had left of her.

My dad was always the jokester, the first to crack a smile and make me laugh. But the hurt in those notebooks, what was with that? Was the happy all an act? I scanned the titles on the shelf, my mind reeling. It had been nearly ten years since she died. What was he protecting me from, and why couldn't we talk about it? She was mine too. Why was he keeping her all to himself?

I found *Charlotte's Web* on the shelf. I took it down and sifted through the browning pages, vaguely remembering reading the book with Dad. I looked inside the cover and saw my mom's name. My fingers traced the light curl of her handwriting, and I thought about her fingers touching the same pages in my hands now, like we were connected by the words in the book. Maybe that's what Dad had felt.

I took a breath, promising myself I wouldn't touch the

notebooks again. They were Dad's private thoughts, and Grandpa always said to respect a man's privacy. Besides, it felt wrong, almost like lying to him—even though I felt like he was lying to me.

I read some of *Charlotte's Web* then carefully placed it back in its slot. I called Dad back. He was just checking in, he said, and wanted to know what I'd like for dinner. I listened close to his voice for the hurt, the pain in those letters, but he sounded normal, just the happy-go-lucky guy he always was.

CHAPTER 7

On the Tuesday before school started, Dad and I drove down to Claremont Middle School for the open house. Dad was in his usual good mood as we sang along with the radio, at least until we pulled into the parking lot and he turned it down.

As he parked the car, I scanned the lot to make sure nobody was watching us. And when Dad turned to me, I could see the sentimental moment reading like a teleprompter in his eyes. "You know I'm really proud of you, right?"

"Yes Dad, thanks," I said, my hand on the door handle. No need to make this more torturous than it was already going to be. Dad grabbed his keys and phone.

"Okay, let's do this," he said. I bolted out of the car.

The school was much bigger than the one back home, but I wasn't thinking much about locker combinations or classes. I couldn't help wondering what Dad might write about our little tour. Lately I'd fallen into a habit of trying to guess what he was thinking or what would make it into the journal. I analyzed everything, like our little moment in the car, wondering what he was going to report back to his notebook.

In the lobby I saw Jaylen from the pool. He broke away from a lady I guessed to be his mom and reached out to give my hand a slap. "High-dive-dude, what's up man?"

"Hey. Jaylen, right?"

"Yep. John?"

"Jack."

"Oh yeah. You didn't go here last year, did you?"

"No, I'm from out of town."

"Yeah, where?"

"Plattsburgh. Upstate New York." I'd taken to saying upstate to limit all of the confusion, but his eyebrows rose anyway.

"I've got an uncle in uh, what's the capital?"

"Albany," Dad inserted.

"Yeah, Albany. And a cousin in Syracuse."

I nodded, looking back to Dad. Our group was leaving the classroom, and out in the hall Jaylen introduced us to his mom. Dad and I followed them down the hall. "So you're in eighth grade?" I asked.

"Yep." He nodded to kids as we passed. As we neared the gymnasium, I heard the shoe squeaks and murmurs of the crowd. Inside, a few groups of parents sat in the bleachers. The basketball hoops were drawn up to the rafters where the sun angled through the windows.

"So, as you probably guessed, this is the gym." He waved a hand across the floor as we walked in. "Now, you have to be careful when it rains. The roof leaks here, and here, and over here." He jumped from spot to spot, still studying the rafters.

"Do you play basketball, like, for the school?" I asked.

He looked at me, cocking his head. "Why? Oh, because I'm black, right?" he said with a smile.

I shook my head, backtracking, heat filling my face. "What? No, I didn't mean..."

He broke into a grin. "Dude, I'm just playing with you. And no, I don't play ball. Not for the school or anywhere else." He tossed up his hands. "Actually, I'm terrible."

"Seriously, I didn't mean—"

His head bounced up. "So what do you do?"

Ski, snowboard, play hockey. None of that mattered down here. Hmm. "Well, I play the drums."

Jaylen's eyes doubled with his smile. "What? Man, for real?"

"Yeah," I said, eyeing him sideways.

"Dude, I play bass!"

I couldn't tell if he was still messing with me or not. "Are you being for real?"

He spun around with a squeak. "Hey, I don't joke about music."

"Okay, cool." This was a guy I could hang with, and before I knew it, I invited him over. "You should come over sometime, my dad plays guitar."

"Okay. Where do you live?"

"On uh, Tre—I mean Crescent View," I stuttered, about to say the old address.

"Okay, yeah, we could do that."

We exchanged numbers. On the way out I was telling Dad I found a bassist when we passed Miranda and her friends again. Megan giggled and tugged on Miranda's arm when she tried to wave. "Hey, Jack."

"Hey Miranda."

Miranda had her hair in a bun. T-shirt, shorts, flip flops. She motioned to Megan—all dressed up in some sort of fancy blouse with textured sleeves.

"So this is Megan. Megan, Jack. Again." Miranda said, sounding a little annoyed.

Dad escaped out to the front steps. Then things got awkward.

"Oh, uh, hey Megan," I said, still looking at Miranda.

Megan turned to another girl and they giggled. Miranda's lips curled into a slight smile, or at least the hint of a smile, followed by the trademark eye roll. Miranda was a top-notch eye roller. And versatile too. She could go left to right, right to left, sometimes just back towards the sky, or down across the floor. I'd seen her do it all summer, mostly at Trevor and his questions, but also when I made a cheesy joke.

When I realized we were just standing there and Megan wasn't going to say anything, I just sort of waved goodbye and ran to catch up with Dad.

"Bye Jack," Miranda said as I reached the door, and I stopped, looked back, and stammered out another goodbye like an idiot. Dad grabbed the door and held it open. Grinning.

"I think she likes you."

I glanced back. "Uh, she's a little weird. What's with all the laughing?"

Dad put an arm on my shoulder. "I meant Miranda."

"Oh." My face went hot, but that could have been Virginia. "What makes you think that?"

"Just a hunch."

When we got home, the old man across the street waved me over to his driveway and introduced himself as Mr. Jacobsen. He offered me twenty bucks to cut his grass each week. And he wanted me to start on the spot. Dad encouraged me and I glanced over the front yard. A few small hills and a couple knotty roots under the oak trees. Cake, right?

Nope. I'd been swindled. The guy's backyard was a beast, long and slanted and rippled with roots, it took me over an hour because his mower was only a spark plug away from being a mule. I wiped my brow, wet and covered with dust. Twenty bucks a cut, yeah, *what a deal.*

I dragged the mule back to the shed, muttering about what Grandpa would call "getting taken for a ride," when I stopped in my tracks as a song drifted through the trees in the woods. I cocked my head, still dripping with sweat and reeking of gas and oil and grass, but my mood lifted by the powerful melody sweeping through the woods like a calming breeze.

Shutting the doors to the shed, I recognized the song, but not the big, confident voice serenading the neighborhood. I wiped my hands on my shorts, taking a seat under the shade of the Chestnut tree in old man Jacobson's backyard, trying to figure out the direction of the voice. A dog barked. The singing stopped, breaking into a laugh I'd heard before.

Miranda's laugh.

CHAPTER
8

I held out for two whole days before I broke the promise I'd made to myself and snuck back into Dad's room. The more I thought about my mom and how little I knew about her, the more I wanted to find out. And she was inside those lined pages of the books inside Dad's closet. I mean, after all, she was *my* mother. Didn't I deserve to know her?

Everything in the new house was different, strange, foreign. It didn't even feel like I was in Dad's room, only some room with his stuff. It wasn't until I had the lid off the box and opened the notebook, when I put the pages to my nose, that it was like he was in the room with me. I sat back, falling into the pages of milestones, like when I rode my bike for the first time.

5-28-13

Jackson rode his bike today. All by himself. I guided him along, and finally, I let go. You should have seen him Ellie, pedaling all by himself. He was so proud.

I smiled, remembering how I kept begging Dad not to let go. When he did I hardly noticed, his hand left my back and I was pedaling away. I flipped through more pages, some stained by wine or coffee. I cocked my head toward the opened door, making sure the house was still. I heard only the faint noises of a summer day. Then I was back in those pages.

I'd found I could tell how my dad was feeling by his handwriting. The way it was always rigid and blocky, bold when he started off, growing messier in some places, fast and excited, or smaller when it was sad or painful, the words spaced out like breaths.

> 7-06-14
>
> *Some guys from work fixed me up on a date. They said it was time. That I was too young to be a widower and I should live some. Jackson stayed with Grandpa, and I felt so guilty I couldn't even tell him. It was a disaster, Ellie. No thanks to you. I swear I heard you laughing at me the whole time. Like when I bumped the table and spilled my drink, or I told that tired story about the cranky bartender in Montreal you've heard me tell a thousand times. But all of my stories involve you. The poor girl, she was nice enough, but my heart wasn't in it.*
>
> *I'm not ready Ellie, I don't think I'll ever be ready...*

I leaned back against his bed and kept reading—about me, about my mom, about a whole side of my dad he'd hidden from me.

> 8-01-17
>
> *Six years without you Ellie. Over 2,100 days, but who's counting, right? Over two thousand nights I've blinked awake reaching for you. I can't even cry anymore, is that bad? At least when I cried I felt something. And now I'm afraid I'm numb to our son. But then I hear him laugh and it's like you're sitting right there. And all I want to do is keep him laughing because his eyes squint like yours did and the more he laughs— your laugh—it's like medicine to my soul.*

The more I read the more I worried. But also the more I wanted to know. Did my dad need real professional help or was this his way of coping? I'd never given much thought about how he felt after Mom died, being depressed or whatever, and now here was a box full of misery sitting in his closet. Kind of scary. Like that last comment, what was that all about? It was like someone else was writing this stuff. Someone I'd never met.

But I enjoyed the entries about Mom. How her eyes shined when she laughed, or how she loved Chinese food and old black and white movies. She liked to sketch and paint, and there were a few of her drawings in the box. She volunteered at the humane society on the weekends. She spent a summer on a farm and even helped bottle feed a baby calf to health. She was allergic to shellfish but loved the ocean more than anything.

Dad wrote about her hair, the arch in her back, her legs, and other really embarrassing stuff I can't mention. But it was clear he loved her very much, like more than anything else in the world. More than me even, I think.

But some of it scared me. Was he really walking around with so much hurt inside? Like this one, for example:

I stopped at Starbucks for coffee today, not sure why. I waited in line behind two women discussing the latest tabloids. I snatched a whiff of Hazelnut coffee and there you were. Suddenly I was in the kitchen, watching you rub your eyes, seeing you in my SUNY Plattsburgh t-shirt. I was there, Ellie. I could feel the warmth of your skin. Just a simple smell and I was transported back. I bought a bag of Hazelnut, just to smell the bag, as though it were a magic potion. But it wasn't. It was just coffee, and you were still gone.

Yeah, I didn't know that guy.

When he came home that evening, tossing his bag on the couch and asking about my day, the guilt hit me like an anvil. He rushed off to change clothes, and in my head I scanned his bedroom floor, panicking because maybe I'd forgotten something, something that would give me away. Worse still, I felt horrible about the sneaking around. Dad always said he wanted us to be open with each other. Well, he'd blown that to bits.

When he shuffled back down the steps, all jokes and smiles, going into some nerd talk story about his day at work, I swallowed hard, shaking off the nagging guilt, laughing it up with him.

Man, I was just as big of a phony as he was.

TREVOR MATERIALIZED at the door as Dad left the next morning. The guy was like my own private rooster. Actually, he had a turkey on his shirt, because apparently Virginia Tech's mascot is Thanksgiving dinner. He wore a flat brim hat down to his eyebrows, so he had to keep lifting it up so he could see.

"Want to ride bikes up to the pool?" he asked.

I thought about all those hills. "The pool. On our bikes?"

"There's a shortcut through the woods," he said, pointing the way. Over his shoulder, I spotted Miranda out in the street breezing around on her bike. A quick jolt of motivation came over me.

"Sure, give me five minutes."

I got my swim trunks on and dug my bike out of the basement. After a quick pump of the tires, I stepped outside where it was warm but not thick-as-butter humid like the late afternoons.

Miranda was way out in front, already up the hill. Trevor and I hung a left on Creekside—another dead end. We hopped the curb and escaped the early morning sun, into the shade on a dirt trail until we arrived at a paved bikeway in the middle of the woods.

The bikeway sliced through the trees, two walls of green pulsing with sound. Catching up with Miranda, I couldn't help peeking at her long legs, smooth and fluid in their motion. We crossed a wooden bridge over the creek and then passed under a giant railroad trestle where Miranda skidded to a stop and turned around.

A few strands of hair escaped from her ponytail and clung to the sweat on her forehead. She narrowed her eyes at me and laughed. "You going to make it?"

I nodded, catching my breath. A woodpecker rattled somewhere in the distance. Trevor slowly plodded around the bend. Miranda called back to her brother, "Trevor, did you bring your inhaler?"

He gasped, shaking his head. Now that we'd stopped, it was clear he was huffing and puffing more than usual. Miranda's mouth tightened. She said something under her breath before she froze. I turned back and found Trevor straddling his bike, hunched over. His face was flushed red, well on its way to purple. Miranda raced back to him, and I followed. She jumped off the bike before it stopped, leaving it to crash as she helped Trevor to the ground.

She whirled around to me. "Wait here with him, I'll be back."

I nodded. Then she was back on her bike, heaving forward, standing up on the pedals and zooming off the way we'd come.

I looked to Trevor, gasping and choking for air. To my amazement, he was trying to calm me down. "Don't worry... I'm okay." He slurred. I nodded and patted his back because I didn't know what else to do. He wheezed and fought for each breath, sucking down mouthfuls of sticky morning air.

Eventually, I motioned to a bench near the bridge and

helped him over. He coughed and hacked like he was choking. Something really bad was happening.

"Trevor, hey Trevor. Look at me buddy." He lifted his head, hissing for breath as I tried to hold his gaze. His chest flung itself up and down and his eyes drifted back in his head.

"Come on buddy, hang in there. I'll even let you play my drums when we get back." I said, looking for Miranda but only finding an empty stretch of road. Trevor nodded, but he was struggling. Birds chirped in the trees, the morning sun speckled the pavement with patterns of light, but I was afraid this kid was dying in my arms.

I was just about to hoist him up on my handlebars when Miranda came flying down the path, her hair waving in the wind. The brakes wrenched as again, she leaped off the bike and ran to us, thrusting the inhaler in her brother's mouth.

"Here Trevvy."

Trevor sucked in a few squirts from the inhaler. I waited for his breathing to return to normal but he was still gagging. Miranda leaned over him, red and sweaty from her mission. Her bathing suit straps poked out from her shirt as she took Trevor's head and again pressed the inhaler to his mouth. "That's it, come on."

A few more spurts down, and he regained some color. Although he still wasn't in great shape. After ten or twenty minutes we got him to his feet and started for home. Me with Trevor's bike and Miranda with her bike on one side and her brother's shoulders on the other. Like that, the three of us limped back to the house.

Mrs. Walker was nearly in tears. She set up a humidifier and threw an oxygen mask on his face. I figured it was time to leave.

I was at the door when Miranda stopped me. "Hey Jack. Thanks."

I nodded. "Is he going to be okay?"

"Yeah, he just needs to rest. His asthma's gotten worse the past few years. But he should be fine."

"Okay, well, I'll come back to check on him," I said, turning for the door.

Miranda touched my arm, her eyes softening with her smile. "Seriously, thank you. It means a lot to me." She let out a small laugh. "And to him. You're all he ever talks about lately."

"Really?" I laughed, shrugging my shoulders. "Well, what can I say?"

With a roll of the eyes she pushed me out the door. "All right, I'll see you later."

CHAPTER 9

8/21/21

It's hard Ellie. Way harder than it was, back when we took turns rocking him to sleep or patting his behind in the wee hours. It's a different kind of hard. He has questions—about school, about girls, about life. Questions you would be able to answer much better than me. He's a good kid. It makes things easier, but still, at times I'm not sure I can keep on.

This was before the transfer. I told him it was a promotion. I had to. But it was take the position or look for work. We've spent our whole lives in Plattsburgh. I could have gotten another job, but it was time to go. I wanted to leave.

Last summer I was jogging at Point Au Roche. I ran out to our spot out at Long Point. I knew what was going to happen before I got there—with the lump climbing up my throat, my eyes watering. By the time I got to the water I lost it. I fell to the ground—at the spot where I proposed, with the waves lapping up on the rocks. The same water that now holds your ashes. I knew I couldn't live like that. It wasn't fair to Jack. Or to me.

It crushes me Jack doesn't have you. I'm not as bitter anymore, but sometimes, when I'm alone, I still feel the anger creeping out.

Because I wish you could see it, Ellie. You would have loved how he's turning out. He has this thing, this simple gesture, this nod he does when he's really excited. It catches my breath. Or when he talks with his hands when he's worked up.

It's you Ellie, all of it. Everything good about Jack is because of you.

The first thing I did when we moved was set the picture of you out on the mantel. My all-time favorite, the one of us at the beach. I did it without thinking. When he noticed, I thought he was going to cry. Our first night in the new house and I'd already blown it.

It's a Sears Home. A craftsman bungalow you would love. It's got this big front porch with a porch swing. Remember how you always wanted a porch swing? I can see you now, curled up with a book, the sun on your shoulders.

Like me, Jack's stubborn. But I think he likes it, not that he'll ever come out and say it! He sulked the entire way down. Yep, I suppose there is some me in him. I can see his eyes flash when he's upset. He has my temper, some of the anger. I know it's hard for him, and I can't console him like you did. The way you could have.

Maybe it was the picture, but I keep thinking about the ocean. The weekend we spent down in North Carolina after college when we had the whole beach house to ourselves and we spent our days in the sand and our nights on the porch listening to the waves. I can still feel you, Ellie, your hair drifting across my face. Your sweet smell, the taste of your neck. Ten years can't take that away from me. No truck can crush those memories or tear them from my mind. They're mine and only mine, Ellie.

Jack and I had a good night, tonight. We jammed in the basement. He's a natural on the drums, we make a great band. I started playing your song, I don't know why, but I did, until I had to stop.

I still miss you, Ellie. I miss you so much it hurts.

I was all messed up after reading that. And he'd just written it, hadn't even bothered to put it in the box. It was on the nightstand under a magazine.

It made me want to scream. *He* was the one who didn't want to talk about her, not me. He said as much in the note—*mine and only mine*. Besides, wasn't he the parent? Didn't this sort of thing fall under his jurisdiction? How was I supposed to just come out and mention it? *Oh Dad, by the way, I've been digging through your deepest, most personal thoughts, and I think you have it all wrong about who doesn't want to bring up Mom.*

I mean, sure, I was scum for sneaking back in there. But then again, here I had all of these beautiful stories about my mom right at my fingertips. How could I resist piecing her together through the journals? Besides, it felt like the only way we could really talk was through those notebooks.

Around five-thirty he came bustling in all smiles and chuckles. "I was thinking we'd order a pizza tonight and then maybe jam some?"

"I'm not feeling it tonight," I said.

He stopped juggling his keys. "You okay?"

"Yeah," I said without looking up from the TV. I was going to tell him about Trevor and his scare earlier, but then he did that low whistle thing, raising his eyebrows like he does when he thinks I'm being grumpy. Whatever, I had every right to be upset with him—whether he knew it or not.

He was the one who'd dragged me away from my friends and brought me down to Virginia where he faked being happy. It wasn't working anymore. The whole thing was an act, and I didn't appreciate it. I sighed and zoned out watching TV, flipping through one show after another without seeing anything. Dad kept on with the whistling. Then he tried another approach.

"Oh, uh, some guys at work said the new Detective Dooger movie is hilarious, I can't remember the actor's name, it's uh…"

Seriously, like that was going to work. I knew his tricks, where acted like he couldn't quite put his finger on something so I'd pipe up with the answer. Nice try Dad, but that scheme wore thin a few years ago. I turned up the volume, but he just kept on talking. "Starts with an S, we were just talking about it. Oh well, hey what do you want on your pizza?"

"Pepperoni's fine."

He held the phone in his hand, staring at the flyer on the fridge. I squirmed, sparring with the meanness growing inside of me. Because what was the plan here, to ignore everything and live off of delivery pizza? And like he said—or, what he wrote— my temper came from him, right? "Hey Dad, the picture up there, with Mom, what beach is that?"

He popped up from the phone, his finger hovering near the buttons. *There*, I thought, digging in. I'd uttered the unspoken word. I was fighting dirty, and it felt horrible and great at the same time. He stared at the wall in the living room until I wanted to take my words back. Then he recovered, looking up from the phone. "Oh, um, it's uh, I think it was Duck, North Carolina."

He *thought*. I was so tired of the games, even if I was the one playing them now. "Oh, okay, because I like that picture."

There, now he knew how I felt. *Ball's in your court, Dad.*

He nodded, blank-faced and still, my words hanging in the room until he held the phone to his ear and walked out to the deck.

I guess I'd won that round. Only it didn't feel like it.

CHAPTER 10

We tagged along with the Walkers again on Saturday night, this time to an outdoor movie at the downtown riverfront. *Goonies* was the feature and Dad was being kind of a spaz, tapping the steering wheel as we followed the Walkers' van downtown. Dad and I had watched *Goonies* like ten times. One of our pastimes was watching old eighties movies and eating junk on the couch on Sundays. At least back home it was.

We arrived around seven-thirty to get a good spot on the lawn. Miranda hopped out wearing jean shorts and a t-shirt. She had her hair down, tucked behind one ear and falling to her shoulder. When she saw us she waved. Not for the first time I wondered how a simple wave could make me dizzy.

Trevor, having regained some color in his face, was back being Trevor again, bouncing around and asking a million questions about a million topics. Mrs. Walker spread out a blanket just as my dad starting tugging at his shirt, already threatening to do the Truffle Shuffle. If you've seen *Goonies* you'd know that right then I had to get far, far away from him.

I started after Miranda, who had wisely put some distance between herself and her parents. "Hey, do you mind if I come with you?" I motioned back to my dad, who waved. Miranda laughed and waved over my shoulder.

"Sure, but you-know-who is coming," she said just as Trevor came bumbling across the grass.

"Hey guys. Wait up."

The three of us strolled through the park. The sweet wafts

of kettle corn hovered over the grounds as a two-piece band strummed along on the sidewalk. We stopped to watch, at least until Trevor—yep, fully recovered from the other day—shuffled around, dancing like his hair was on fire. Miranda rolled her eyes and stormed off.

The sky flared orange and red, then falling purple as the lamp posts flickered to life. Trevor walked in the middle as Miranda texted her friends. I pulled out my phone and fiddled around.

Miranda laughed. "Oooh, look who got a phone!"

I shrugged like it was no big deal, but she reached over Trevor's head and snatched it from me, turning away to read the text I was typing.

"Hey, give it back."

She giggled, staring at the screen. "'Will, what's up dude?'" she said in a deep mimicking voice. "Wow, important stuff going on."

"Ha ha. Now, give it."

"Maybe I should text Will, let's see here…"

"Give it."

"Oh, how I miss you, Will."

I lunged for the phone and Miranda squealed. She took off, running out onto the field, her arm stretched as she held my phone away. "Miranda, give it back!" I yelled, even though I couldn't stop smiling as I chased after her through a gust of berries.

Trevor wobbled after us. Miranda broke away and I set after her all over again. Her long strides were impossible to match. She galloped toward the portable toilets, and a woman startled, pulling her dog close. Miranda shifted, changed direction, then darted behind the stalls, peeking out with a smile.

When I ran one way, she looped back around, giggling between breaths until I took the angle and gained on her, ignoring the lady with the dog who yelled at me as I hopped her leash.

Just as I had Miranda within reach, she ducked behind a tree and slung herself back toward the field. I wheeled around the tree, catching a gust of berries as she spun around. I couldn't stop. I grabbed her arms, and she turned and faced me and I wasn't really sure what to do next. I lunged ahead and her eyes lit up with laughter, quick and hot on my face as my phone fell to the ground.

"Whoa, you two okay?" A man wearing a hat stood to the side with two small, hip-high children at each hand. A little dog barked at us as we both stared at the man for a moment until I realized our hands were still clasped together.

"Yeah, sorry," Miranda said to the man, breaking away from me just as Trevor finally caught up to us.

I snatched my phone off the ground and brushed myself off when a girl's voice called out. "Miranda, *what* are you doing?"

A blonde girl stared at us like we were crazy. Three boys around my age stood with bored looks on their faces. Well, not counting the cocky one with the really short spiky hair and light green polo shirt. He was kind of glaring at us.

"Oh, nothing, we were just, nothing. Jack this is Kaylee, Kaylee, this is Jack." Miranda's voice sounded off. I'd never seen her flustered, but I couldn't tell if she was flushed from the running or the sudden company.

Kaylee shot me a smirk. I waved, still catching my breath. Kaylee turned back to Miranda. "Well, hey, we're going to grab something to eat at the stand. You want to come?"

Miranda shrugged. "Oh, um, sure, I guess. Trevor, tell Dad I'll be over at the picnic tables, I'll be back in a few."

"But you're going to miss the movie," Trevor said, and Spike Hair snorted, prompting snickers from the group.

Kaylee waved to us. "Bye Jack, it was nice meeting you." Miranda joined them as they started off.

"Who are they?" I asked once they were out of earshot. I tried to sound uninterested as I watched Miranda brush back her hair and whisper to Kaylee, who shot me a look then covered her mouth as she giggled.

"Kaylee and Miranda used to be really good friends, but they don't really hang out anymore. The tall guy is Brice Wilkes; he's on the football team. All the girls like him. He lives out in Pinehurst on the golf course, near the country club and stuff."

"Yeah well, he seems like a tool."

Trevor cracked up. "Yeah, he *is* a tool."

As soon as the sun went down, the big movie screen flashed to life. A stupid cartoon kicked things off. Trevor and I edged along the blankets spread out on the field, finding our parents. I plopped down beside Dad on the grass because we hadn't thought ahead to bring a blanket. Every so often I'd casually twist around to get a glimpse at Miranda and her friends sitting over at the picnic tables. The Brice guy sat up on the table, his feet on the bench, his cocky grin irritating me even from fifty yards away.

The half-moon hung overhead, lending a glow to the night, and the heat was bearable. I sighed. Being the new kid in the eighth grade was going to be a blast. I really didn't care what people thought of me, but when I looked over and saw Miranda and Brice had gotten up and were walking together under the light posts, I felt an empty pit in my stomach.

The movie cranked up, and I think Mr. Walker and Dad were more excited than anyone else. Dad whistled as the opening credits rolled. I tried to get into the movie but I was lost in my own thoughts. And I was still lost when Miranda showed up, nudging Trevor out of the way and finding a spot on the blanket beside me. With a huff she stretched her legs out, then huffed again as she stole some of Trevor's popcorn and drink, smacking him on the leg when he whined.

I tried to watch the movie, but then Miranda stretched out and gathered her hair and set it on her head. Then she leaned back and her hand brushed against mine. I jerked my hand away but then I wished I hadn't. Okay, so maybe I did care what one person thought. Maybe it was her eyes, or her long legs, or the way one side of her mouth rose higher when she smiled. I didn't know what it was exactly; I just knew everything felt better with her around.

CHAPTER 11

D ad got called into work the next morning—something to do with a server crashing. I scarfed down some Frosted Flakes, gave it about thirty seconds of thought, then bolted for the closet.

I only made it a few pages. Just wasn't in the mood for it. Sometimes it was a drag, reading about my dad's broken heart and all. But then something clicked. Having read about how my mom loved the beach and painting so much, I had a hunch. I shut the notebook and bounced down the steps to Dad's office.

On the wall hung the only painting in our house. A pier at the beach. Nothing fancy, some fishermen set against a sunset. It had hung in Grandpa's office back home in a simple wooden frame, one of those things I'd passed by so many times without a second glance. But not today. Today I noticed the initials scrawled at the bottom: *E.L.*

And just like that, a simple painting became brand new to me. I imagined my mom's hands holding the brush, swiping those perfect strokes so many years ago, before I was born. The purple streaks in the belly of the clouds, the pink sunset, the ripples in the water—maybe it wasn't so simple after all.

Dad came home and hopped right on a conference call, which had to be one of the most boring things I've ever heard in my life. Top five for sure.

Well going forward, I think... Yes, Bob's working on the upgrade... Did he get the meeting invite? Let's discuss the Willard situation..."

I couldn't even bear to listen anymore. I slapped on my headphones and hit the trails on my bike, just kind of thinking things through. But my mind wasn't ready to let Mom go.

The painting lingered in my head as I rode the bikeway where Trevor had his asthma attack. Were there more? Did Dad bring them down here? Does he stash them away like the notebooks, hiding them from me?

Sometimes it was nice to turn my brain off for a while and drift. But it was tough to do with all the new developments scrambling around in there. Dad and his secrets. How we'd moved and left Grandpa. Miranda and the way she looked at me and smiled. I pedaled ahead, and by the time I stopped I was downtown at the riverfront.

I stared at the empty stage of the amphitheater, leaning forward and resting my arms on the handlebars. I'd read that Mom and Dad were really into music. In the journals, Dad had mentioned how they loved this singer/songwriter, Yari Parker. They'd been to five or six of her concerts. Their wedding song was "Forever" by her, and I'd read about how she'd played it at their first concert together when Mom was in college. They had front row seats, but I'm not sure Dad even saw the concert the way he wrote about Mom.

When I got back, Dad was done with his conference call. He announced tacos were on the menu and made me give him a dorky fist bump. I did, and I had to admit it was nice to be normal for a while.

We did it spicy. Dad diced up jalapenos while CCR rambled through the speakers. I used to tease him about his old music, but I guess jamming together over the years had taught me to appreciate the classics. I could never stay upset with my dad for too long, not with the way he bopped around the kitchen. And pretty soon we were both dancing around, singing. Still, he noticed things.

"So uh, you okay?" he asked as we sat down. I looked over the colorful dinner spread out before us and actually thought about making a full confession as "Fortunate Son" faded out. But after his conference call, all the thinking I'd done, and school starting tomorrow—it didn't seem like the time for such an epic discussion.

"Yeah, I'm cool," I said, stuffing my face. Because right then, with the two of us, on taco night—things were okay.

He nodded, a soft taco leaking from his hand. "A little nervous about tomorrow?"

I wiped my face and shrugged. "I guess, a little maybe."

Honestly, I didn't know what to expect. I had a couple classes with Miranda, but I was determined not to go chasing her around like Trevor did with me. Besides, if she hung out with those guys from the movies—guys like Brice—I'd better stay clear anyway.

That night in bed, all the stuff I'd put out of my mind at dinner came back to haunt me. Along with some new worries. Like how I'd hardly heard from Will and the rest of the guys back home. How my spot on the hockey team was as good as gone, probably like my place at the lunch table.

Man, I wondered if my old friends even noticed I was gone.

CHAPTER 12

"Jack, get up. It's ten after seven."

I rolled into the wall, buried my head under my pillow, still able to hear my dad's deep bellow in the doorway. Something about school. Oh yeah. School.

I tore the sheet off and hopped out of bed, nearly flying backwards as my feet rolled over the drumsticks in route to the bathroom.

Dad popped his head out of his doorway, fixing his belt. "Easy there, cowboy. I can give you a ride if you need it."

After a super quick shower, I toweled my hair dry, found my favorite pair of jeans, and wrestled a Plattsburgh State Cardinals t-shirt over my head. It was seven-thirty by the time I dumped sugar over my Cheerios. Dad sat down at the table with his iPad.

"Guess who stopped by while you were in the shower?"

"Miranda?" I asked with a little too much hope in my voice.

"Trevor."

"Oh."

Dad set down the iPad and looked me over. "I can't believe you're in the eighth grade already."

"It's too early for corniness, Dad."

"Never. But I could take you to school, give you a noogie, maybe give you a kiss on the cheek if you want?"

I pretended to mull it over. "I think I'll take my chances on the bus."

I wolfed down my cereal and hiked to the bus stop where I

found Trevor, his stiff-as-cardboard jeans rolled up at his ankles. He was talking with another munchkin and his shirt was tucked in and buttoned to the collar. I wondered how Miranda let him leave the house dressed like that. Speaking of Miranda, she wasn't around.

Trevor saw me and pounced. "Hey Jack. Tell Zack we jam together in the band."

The Zach kid was all wide eyed and gullible. Too easy. I nodded. "Oh yeah, for sure. And Trevor holds it all together. There would be no band without Trev."

The kid's mouth fell open. He looked at his friend with newfound amazement. "Cool."

I smiled, happy to do the favor. At least someone thought I was cool. Trevor nodded, gave the kid a *told you so* look, and then they were off into a heated discussion with another runt about a fantasy book involving trolls and spells and all sorts of other hideous nerd stuff. I nodded, plugged in my ear buds, and let Rush bang on my ear drums until the bus rolled to a stop.

Climbing aboard, the bus smelled like onions and feet. I found an empty seat near the middle, and Trevor plopped down one seat behind me with his buddy. A quick blast from his inhaler, and he continued yapping about fantasy land.

"So after that, the knights storm the mountain to where the princess is locked away, and..."

I stared out the window, thinking about back home, where they started school in September like normal people. It was still summer break for another month. And when school did start, I'd know everyone and wouldn't be starting completely over.

At the school, me and my two sixth grade buddies milled about the entrance near the trees. I scanned the groups. The popular kids were easy to sort out, all confidence and laughing. The jocks, the loners, the losers—even a squad of dorks came sauntering past, carrying loaded down bags and instrument cases, stopping to talk to Trevor and Zach.

Trevor called after me. "We're going to the cafeteria, you want to go?"

"No, I'm good. Thanks."

"Okay, see ya around."

I set off to find my locker, getting lost and looping around the hallway. The first bell rang, putting me on the clock. Back tracking, I checked my phone out of habit.

"Lost?"

I looked up to find Miranda, her hair twisting and curling to her shoulders. She smiled at me, and I stuffed my phone in my pocket.

"No, I just..."

"You're totally lost, aren't you?"

"I think, I just—" I looked left, then right. "Yep."

Miranda laughed, nodding her head to the right. "Mrs. Dabney's class is this way, come on." Her eyes seemed extra bright and warm, inviting me to stare. We started back the way I'd come then went left.

"So how was the bus?"

I groaned.

She smirked. "Did Trevor talk your head off?"

"Well..."

"Let me guess, they talked the whole time about dragonslaying and princess-rescuing?"

I laughed. "Yep."

As we walked, nearly everyone who passed said hello or waved to Miranda. Miranda waved back, not just to the obviously popular kids but also giving a little boost to the ones looking unsure of themselves.

She pointed the way, and I found my locker just outside our classroom. "Here you are."

In class, kids scattered to find familiar faces to sit near. Miranda nodded to a desk near the back and we sat down just before the bell. Mrs. Dabney welcomed us to our first day at Claremont Middle before the morning announcements crackled through the ancient speaker. A voice I recognized welcomed us to THE FIRST DAY OF SCHOOL!!!

After class, Miranda filled me in on how Megan hosted the announcements as she guided me toward the computer labs. From there I was on my own. I caught a few stares in the hallway, but it didn't bother me because I wasn't there to impress anybody. Besides, if things went well—meaning if I made Dad miserable enough—I should be home by next semester.

Entering the cavernous darkness of computer science, I took a seat at an empty desk, setting my bag on the floor amongst the wires and plugs, when I heard a familiar voice.

"Yo, High Dive."

Jaylen slid down beside me with a smile. I had to admit, it was nice to see another familiar face. "What's up Jaylen. You work up the courage to jump off yet?"

"All you, my man."

The desks around us filled, and soon the bell rang and Mr. Coleman shut the door and took inventory of the class. He wore a yellow button-down short sleeve shirt and looked *exactly* like someone you'd peg for a guy who taught computer science. I mean, yeah, my dad worked with computers but at least he played guitar to balance things out. Mr. Coleman dimmed the lights and began, in an automated tone, to go over the class syllabus. When Jaylen began fake snoring I covered my face. This was not going to end well.

Turned out, both Jaylen and I had second lunch. He waved me over, and I found a place to sit along with two taller kids, one of which I remembered from the pool. I thought it might be okay until Miranda and Megan walked by with two other girls I didn't recognize. I played it cool, so I thought, not knowing how Miranda would be around her friends. But Megan was already doing her giggling thing.

Miranda gave me a quick wave. "Hey Jack."

"Hey."

Jaylen's face lit up. He waited until they passed and smirked.

"What?" I asked.

"Dude, you know Miranda and Megan?"

"Yeah, well, Miranda lives down the street from me," I said, keeping my voice low. He just kind of grinned.

"Miranda's cool man. Megan too."

The way he said Megan's name made me chuckle. "You um, you like Megan?"

Jaylen's grinned widened. "Yeah, I mean, she helped me out in science class last year." He glanced back at her in a way I knew meant he was interested in more than science.

Miranda and Megan sat at the "cool" table with Brice and the rest of the kids from the movies the other night. I noticed Miranda wasn't really sitting *with* Brice but at the other end of the table. She glanced up and I turned back to Jaylen. "That Brice guy, what's his deal?"

"Pfft, he just thinks since he's the quarterback and all, everybody is sweating him. You know how that goes..."

I nodded, staring off at the table. "You think Miranda likes him?"

Then Jaylen was the one laughing. "Uh oh, new guy's already crushing hard."

That afternoon on the bus I received a full recap of Trevor's day. Every class he was in, his teachers, I even found out what he had for lunch—peanut butter and banana. I'd mostly tuned him out though, and when he finally stopped talking I squeezed in a question.

"So what time does Miranda usually get home?"

"Huh? Oh, I think around four."

"You guys want to come over and jam?"

"Yesss! I'll tell her as soon as she gets home. And I'll bring my trumpet."

CHAPTER 13

Miranda didn't show. But when Dad got home a little after five he rushed down to the basement, stripping down to a t-shirt, asking about my day until he saw Trevor holding a trumpet. His eyes widened. "We have a horn section now?"

Trevor launched into his pitch. "It's the only instrument I know. I'm tired of the tambourine."

"Do you actually *play* the trumpet?" I asked.

"Well, I don't just carry it around to look cool."

I shook my head. "That's for sure."

Dad shrugged. "Okay then, let's hear it."

We barreled into "Heartbreak" by Led Zeppelin. After some fiddling and adjustments, Trevor chimed in, which was, if nothing else, interesting. I looked at Dad who squeezed his eyes shut to keep from losing it. We sounded like Miles Davis—if he were deaf.

Then Dad stopped, seemingly lost in thought for a moment. He tuned a string and then looked to Trevor. "Hey Trevor, why don't you play something, anything. We'll follow your lead."

Trevor beamed, his fingers dancing on the buttons of his horn. He put his lips to the mouthpiece, gave us a little smirk, then plowed into a bumpy version of "Rock Around the Clock." Dad followed in behind him with a riff, and finally I found a beat. It still sounded awful, but better.

It was a good time. In fact, we had so much fun I didn't

realize it was after seven until Miranda came down calling for her little brother. She hopped off the last step, eyes wide, obviously amused at the sight of our little three-piece band. When Dad saw her, he never missed a chord, smiling and motioning to the microphone. She shook her head, but Dad kept playing, pointing the guitar to the mic stand and coaxing her forward.

She fixed her hair, stepped forward, and tapped the microphone. "Testing, testing."

She jerked away at the feedback. Dad made a quick adjustment on the fly then looped back into "Rock Around the Clock."

Miranda shrugged. We played on for another minute or two until she regained her courage. Only this time she started singing.

And she blew us away.

Soon as she started, I nearly dropped my sticks. Dad missed a chord because he had to pick his jaw up from the floor. The power in her voice was amazing, but at the same time controlled and smooth. She didn't know all the words, but we kept looping the song over and over again. And the more comfortable she became, the more she let it go. And the more she let go, the more all the noise began to sound like a real song.

Dad screeched to a halt, wiping his eyes. "Wow, you can sing!"

Miranda laughed, waving him off. But Dad was more excited than I'd seen him in a while. We played riffs and Miranda sang pop songs over them. She could have sung a Surgeon General's warning for all I cared. But then she dug in her pocket and found her phone.

We all stopped playing. She motioned to Trevor. "We've got to go, Trev."

Poor Trevor was starting to wheeze some anyway. We trooped upstairs where Dad and I walked them out to the porch. Afterwards, Dad shut the door and turned to me. "Wow."

"Right?" I told him how I'd heard her behind Mr. Jacobsen's house, he shook his head in amazement as I followed him to the kitchen where he cut into a mound of bread for Italian paninis.

He asked about school again, bouncing from the fridge to the counter. I shrugged.

"It wasn't that bad. I've got lunch with Jaylen, and Computer class."

"What about Miranda, don't you have a class with her, too?"

"Yeah, but..." I told him about Brice and the lunch table. Dad looked at me quizzically.

"High drama on the first day, huh?" he said, bringing over our plates to the table. "Hot plate."

I shrugged, biting into my sandwich and blistering the roof of my mouth.

"Ahhhh!"

"Hot. Plate."

Dad grabbed two Sprites and plopped back down. He took a bite, chewed, then his face lit up like he just remembered something. "Oh yeah, so uh, next Friday, Yari Parker is coming to Charlottesville, about an hour away. You want to go?"

I coughed, choking on the burn and the soda and the room-spinning coincidence of the words "Yari Parker" coming out of his mouth after I'd read his notebooks. Was it a test? I wiped my mouth before glancing back at Dad, who stared at me like I was crazy.

"You're having some time with dinner tonight. You okay?"

I nodded. "Yeah, yeah."

"So do you want to go? It's a Saturday night."

I managed a nod. Dad talked about work, some project they

were working on. But I didn't pay attention. Didn't eat much. I was too busy thinking how maybe this concert would be our big breakthrough.

CHAPTER 14

After school on Tuesday, I did battle with Mr. Jacobsen's yard. I'd slacked off over the weekend, so I had to mow the backyard twice where the grass brushed my ankles. Trudging along, I caught the old man watching, peering from his window like a prison guard. When he saw me looking he motioned to a spot I'd missed.

All for twenty bucks.

At least cutting grass gave me time to think about the day, starting with the bus ride with Trevor and his insistence on explaining the Harry Potter series in painstaking detail. Then I'd passed Miranda in the hallway, with her cool crowd, Brice looming over her shoulder, smirking at me as they walked by. Whatever, I wasn't going to beg the guy to let me hang out with them. I hockey-sneered back at him until he turned away and whispered something to his buddies.

A few thick drops of rain hit my forearms. The sky was thick with mean dark clouds and threatening to dump. Fine by me, I was in the mood for a good storm.

I released the mower handle. The engine sputtered and conked. My hands still vibrated from lugging the machine over the yard several hundred times. Mr. J came out to lower his flag from the pole and, after pointing out several spots he wanted raked, he begrudgingly handed over a wrinkled twenty. I stuffed the bill in my pocket then returned his mower as a gust of wind hurled and nearly took the door off the shed. The leaves on the trees flipped over white, and I could almost taste the storm. I locked up and hustled across the street, the rain picking up as I found Dad on the porch.

"I think you just made it," he said, tossing me a bottle of water. Sheets of rain slammed down sideways. I kicked off my grassy shoes and peeled off my sweaty socks, taking a seat on my chair and feeling the water bouncing off the front of the porch as the storm blew in.

"I love a good storm," Dad said, and I nodded in agreement. The rain hit the street in waves, gushing down the hill in ripples. Thunder clapped overhead, and we sat in silence, enjoying the downpour. Until we heard someone yelling.

"Waaaaaallly!"

Dad and I jumped up, heads craning toward the Walkers' house. "Is that Miranda?"

Had to be. Who else had a voice you could hear over a storm? I peeked out from the porch, rain pelting the back of my head. Miranda was out in the street, shielding her face with her hands, ducking under bushes and around the trees.

"Waaaaaally! Here boy!"

I leaped off the steps and ran down the street, my bare feet slapping the wet asphalt. Miranda turned, wiping her eyes and slicking her hair back. "Wally's scared of storms. I have to find him!" she yelled, squinting in the rain.

"Any idea where he'd go?"

She looked left then right then shrugged. "Maybe at the camp." Thunder boomed overhead and we both jumped. She laughed then motioned to the woods. "I'm going to check."

We hit the Walkers' driveway, bounding for the woods, Miranda's shoes squishing in the puddles, flecks of mud spotting her ankles and calves with her steps. We looked in the trees and under a shed, calling out for Wally as the sky boomed and rain poured.

We came down to the clearing, past the fire pit with

benches and kettles, a zip line stretched overhead from two large trees with wooden chairs set aside in the tall grass. I followed Miranda to the large screened in gazebo. Stepping in, she wiped her face with her hand. Out there, dripping wet, she looked smaller than she did at school, vulnerable even.

Deer antlers hung overhead, a couple of dusty lanterns and some fishing lures sat on a small wooden table. Miranda stared out into the storm, calling for Wally again.

"I hope he's okay," she said, her hands on her hips. I wiped the mud from my legs and Miranda smiled at my feet. "You're not even wearing shoes."

I shrugged, and we stood there, both drenched as the rain let up from downpour to steady. Miranda spanned the woods with a nervous eye.

"This is a cool spot. Do you guys camp down here a lot?" I asked, looking over the wicker furniture, the cushions damp from all the rain.

She stepped back from the screen. "Not as much anymore. You should have seen this place when Trevor was in Cub Scouts though," she said with a laugh. "We're trying to get Dad to have a big neighborhood campout this fall."

"Cool."

She smiled, peeking up at me. "One time, I told Trevor I'd seen a bear down here, and he refused to come back for a month."

"That's funny," I said with a laugh. "But you didn't really see a bear, I mean...did you?"

"Maybe." She wiggled her eyebrows, then called for Wally again.

The storm moved quickly. Soon the thunder only grumbled in the distance, fading as the leaves fluttered in the drizzle. The creek was high from the wash out, swirling, with sticks and limbs in its current. Miranda squeezed her hair and the water dripped onto the floor. She took a seat on the chair and looked over to me. "So, if you don't mind me asking, like, what happened to your mom?"

I wiped my mouth, breaking free from her gaze to the wet footprints on the dusty floor of the gazebo. It was weird, her coming out with that, because lately I'd sort of wanted to talk out loud about Mom. I looked up. "Well. She got hit by a tractor trailer. A logging truck coming through the mountains. The weather was bad. Ice, fog, and stuff."

Miranda's eyes widened with sympathy. I told the scattered details of what I knew about my mom's accident. Usually I stopped there, but down in the woods with the rain, the storm, Miranda—I kept going. "I was only three and would have been with her, but I was sick that day and with my dad."

She closed her eyes and whispered, "I'm so sorry."

I shrugged, part of me feeling like I'd said too much but also wanting to keep talking. I liked this Miranda, the one in the woods, soaking wet, away from school and the quarterback at lunch.

"I don't remember her at all. All I know of her is what I see in pictures and stuff. It's just been my dad and me ever since."

She nodded, like she understood. Like, really understood, as if she was reading my mind. I turned to the screen and looked out to the woods. The rain had stopped but it was hard to tell by the way the trees were dripping. Miranda stood and looked out to the woods before she turned back to me. "Well, in case you haven't noticed, I'm adopted."

I shrugged as though I hadn't. "Oh, I just..."

She laughed a little. "It's okay, really. We get lots of looks at restaurants and stuff. It's like people wonder if my dad cheated on my mom or the other way around."

"So you don't know your real parents?"

She turned to me like she didn't understand the question.

"Well, yeah, I live with my real parents. I mean, they're all I've ever known."

"Sorry, I didn't mean it like that."

"No, it's okay." She looked down to her wet footprints on the dry wooden planks as she paced. "My mom and dad were told they couldn't have kids. They adopted me as soon as I was born. My birth mother was only sixteen. Anyway, they took me home, and a year and a half later, a miracle happened." She looked up and smiled. "Or whatever you want to call Trevor."

The sun fought to break free of the clouds. Miranda seemed to sense my questions. "It's just, when I was little I thought I was different, you know—different than my family. It was like I didn't fit in anywhere, like I was too white for black people and too black for white people. But now?" she shrugged. "I don't know. I'm proud of who I am."

The confidence had returned to her voice, a sort of pride that made me smile. And without thinking I blurted out. "So, I'd heard you sing, before the other night, when I was cutting grass at Mr. J's."

She turned to me with a smirk. "You spying on me or something?"

"No, I was just... I was at Mr. Jacobsen's. I didn't mean to..."

She laughed. "No, it's okay. But next time cover your ears."

"Why? You're amazing. I mean, your singing is amazing. I mean you are too, it's just—"

Miranda waved her hands to shut me up. "Jack. Thanks."

"Yeah. So um, are you in chorus or something?"

She sighed. "No, my mom's been pushing for me to sing all my life, church choir, chorus, that kind of stuff. But I just like to do my own thing. Does that make sense?"

"Completely," I said, then I opened my mouth again to say something stupid when there was a bark in the distance.

Miranda leaped up from the chair, her eyes wide and wonderful.

"Wally!"

She turned and shot out of the gazebo. I followed, the screen door slamming shut as we sprinted for a patch of bamboo trees near the bank where the creek frothed and splashed, slapping rocks on the embankment. Wally barked again, and I followed Miranda into the thick trees.

"Wally, come here boy."

Wally let out a whimper, his tail swishing as he rose from his hiding place. Miranda smiled like a little girl as he raced over to her, happy and tail wagging as he pranced all the way home.

CHAPTER 15

I set my head against the window. Hay bales and tractors blurred into a kaleidoscope of color as Route 29 lay stretched out in front of us. Mom was on my mind, the mountains in the background, and every few miles Dad would snap me from my thoughts with a question about school or music. When he did I forced myself to be in the moment with him. Yari Parker, here we come.

The outdoor mall in Charlottesville was kind of like Church Street in Burlington, with shops and restaurants and couples roaming the sidewalks. Street singers and poets performed at every bench or table. We hit up Five Guys for dinner, where I talked Dad into getting extra jalapenos on his cheeseburger.

I nearly spit out my drink watching him gag and sweat after taking down two back to back. He sucked up three root beers and I was still choking with laughter as he leaned back in his chair, wiping his forehead with his napkin.

I nodded to his tray. "You still have a jalapeno to go."

He grimaced, picked it up, then took it down in dramatic fashion, nodding his head as he swallowed. Then came the inevitable Dad talk. "So now that you've got your first week under your belt, how is it? Are you going to survive?"

I sipped my root beer, thinking it through. If I really wanted to pack up and go home to crash with Grandpa, this was it. Now was the time. But how would that work? Sure, I loved my grandpa and all, but he went to bed at eight o'clock every night. And besides, who was I kidding? I wasn't going to leave Dad. I snatched a french fry and drenched it in ketchup. "Yeah, I think so."

He smiled, took a breath, and wiped his forehead. I thought a speech was coming, but he was sweating from the heat of the jalapenos. He slapped the table with his palm. "Okay, I need a drink refill."

After dinner we hiked to the amphitheater and got through the gates just as the opening act took the stage. The place was cool, with a large tent-like backdrop behind the band to capture the sound. The opening band was good, they had a fiddler and a banjo and the girl could really sing. Dad got a beer, and we wandered around looking for a spot in the grass.

The sky was a washboard of orange and pink clouds. We found a place on the grass beside a couple with a baby. Then, reading from the script I'd written in my head on the way up, I started asking questions. "Have you seen Yari Parker before?"

He nodded, took a swig of beer. "Yeah, a few times, but it's been a while."

According to the journals, it was twelve years ago. I was about to ask if he and Mom went together when the crowd erupted.

The stage pulsed with colorful lights while the roadies scurried onstage to take down and set up. I scoped out the drum set, thinking how cool it would be to hit the road and tour with a band. Overhead, the sky was dark with only a hint of light on the horizon over the bridge. Dad kept his eyes on the stage, his face deep in thought. He was probably thinking about Mom. Stupid as it sounds, it sort of felt like she was with us, and thinking about that, another wave of prickles fell over my skin.

The stage went dark. Four figures emerged from the shadows. A couple clicks and then a buzz hit the air. Dad put his arm around me and squeezed my shoulder. I let him have a cheesy moment because honestly, I was feeling it too.

The lights flashed and there she was. We had a great line of view, just at the ropes before the seated section. Yari Parker waved to the packed crowd and took a seat with her guitar on her knees. *One, two, one, two, three, four...*

The drums crashed and the guitar wailed. Cell phones lit the way to the stage as heads bobbed and bounced into a frenzy. Dad did that really loud whistle with his fingers in his mouth and tiny Yari Parker played the slide guitar like I'd never heard before. It was amazing, the ease in which she squeezed sounds out of the instrument in her lap. We swayed and cheered and rocked with the crowd. The faces were young and old, a mix of color and culture. I kept looking over to Dad because he had a mile-wide smile plastered on his face.

Toward the end of the show things slowed down. Switching guitars, Yari came out on stage by herself and played some acoustic tunes. I immediately recognized the words to "Angel from Montgomery." The lights from the stage hit my Dad's face. He was singing every word like no one else was there. After an encore, and then another, the band took a bow on stage, I screamed and cheered until I was hoarse. When it was all over, it was like I'd been grabbed and shaken by the music then set back down to figure it out for myself. My ears rang, my legs bounced, and my face felt like rubber from smiling.

It was nearly eleven thirty by the time we got on the highway. In the darkness of the car I felt hidden from Dad, and my thoughts roamed back to the journals. I took a breath. "Did you and Mom go to a lot of concerts?"

A car passed and Dad made a sound in his throat. The taboo word had been spoken. "Well, uh, yeah I suppose. We liked most of the same kinds of music. She loved Yari Parker."

This was my chance. We drove another mile or two in silence, and I fought and squirmed to get it out. To tell my own dad how I'd read his letters, his confessions to his wife. To my mom. The words were right there on my tongue. All I had to do was just let them free. That would be the only way we'd stop being so weird about her.

But I didn't. I just sat there like a dunce. The moment passed and the miles of silence repaired the wall I'd only cracked and not shattered.

It was after one by the time we pulled into our driveway. Walking inside, it felt like home. With our stuff, our smells, our secrets.

I changed clothes and got into bed, my head still buzzing from the night of fun and music. Dad's light stayed on, glowing beneath his closed door. I knew he was in there writing to my mom, spilling all of those thoughts he kept hidden from me. I had to talk to him. I'd been so close.

Maybe tomorrow.

CHAPTER 16

On Monday at the bus stop, Trevor was blabbing about his top ten Marvel movies when Miranda came strolling up the street.

"Hey dorks."

Trevor turned around. "What are *you* doing here?"

"Mom has an appointment and can't take me today, guess I'm stuck with you."

Jacob Thomas, a spazzy seventh grader, blew a good-sized snot rocket from his nose. Miranda's jaw fell open. "Oh, how wonderful." She turned to me. "So this is what I've been missing?"

"And the burping contests, you've missed those too," I added.

"Nice."

We boarded the bus, I took my usual seat in row fourteen, and she crashed in the seat behind me. Our bus was never filled, and today was no different. Trevor sat with Zach and they discussed all things nerd. Miranda peeked over the seat, her bright eyes settling on me. "Hey, so uh, I've got bad news."

"Yeah?"

"I think Megan's officially moved on. Looks like you're old news now."

I turned, set one hand on the back of the seat, the other to my heart. "I'm crushed."

She set her hand on mine with mock sympathy. "You've lost your chance. Are you going to be okay?"

I shook my head, wiped my eyes, trying my best to ignore her hand on mine. "I think so, life will go on."

She laughed, flopping back into her seat. I went to turn around when I remembered. "Oh, well, since she has moved on, maybe you could ask her what she thinks about Jaylen?"

She raised her eyebrows. "Jaylen Carter? Huh." She shrugged. "Maybe."

"I mean, I'll be eternally jealous of course."

"Yeah, but, hmm. Hey, why don't you guys eat lunch with us today? We can see what happens." Her mouth turned up in a devilish grin.

"Uh..."

That meant eating lunch with Brice, not high on the list of things I was dying to do. I guess my face gave away my thoughts because she tilted her head. "What, you can't eat lunch with me?"

"No, I mean, yes. I mean..."

She laughed and it was settled. Off the bus I wandered to my locker in a daze, rattled by Miranda's invitation. Because even though I'd rather swallow thumbtacks than eat lunch with Brice and his little crew, I wasn't stupid enough to turn down an invitation to eat lunch with Miranda.

I found Jaylen before class and we talked more about him coming over to jam, but before I got a chance to mention the new seating arrangement at lunch he pulled out a wrinkled flyer from his back pocket. "Hey, check this out."

I glossed over the colorful flyer, some sort of charity contest. "Fall Bash?"

"Yeah, it's a big fund raiser they do every year downtown. Check it."

The flyer listed band names competing for donations to causes of their own choosing. Several slots were still available. I handed it back to him.

"And you're showing me this, why?"

"What? Because we should enter."

"Dude, these are like real bands, we've never even played together."

"Well, first of all, that's why we need to get practicing," he said, shaking the flyer for emphasis. "Second, it's not a contest, it's a fundraiser."

He had a point. "Let me see it again." October fifteenth gave us a little less than two months to practice. I shot Jaylen a suspicious look. "You any good?"

"Pfft, I don't wanna brag, but, yeah. I can come over this weekend and we can get this thing started."

"Okay, let's do it." Then, thinking what Trevor might say, I added. "But we're not a band."

"We'll see. Look, we still have time. What do we have to lose?"

His enthusiasm was contagious. And besides, it would be nice to jam. That settled, I shot him a smile. "So uh, what are you doing for lunch?"

In the cafeteria, we groveled our way toward Brice's table. Miranda saw us coming and waved us over. Brice and his buddies—Danny Ferrell and Ryan Somebody, both watched with suspicious scowls.

We found a spot down at the end of the table where Miranda, Megan, and Kaylee laughed about the mysteries of the world. Brice was at the other end of the table with his smug smile. I stared him down until he looked away.

"Hey guys," Miranda said, making room for us. Jaylen glanced back at our old table, where Freddie and Jay glared at us with betrayal in their eyes. I think Jaylen felt as out of place as me. Especially when Brice got up from his spot and slid a chair up to our end of the table.

"What's up fellas?" he said, reeking of arrogance.

"What's up?" I grumbled. He'd never spoken directly to me, but I guess my entering his territory made him chatty.

"So, Jack. You're from Canada, right?"

"No," I said without looking at him.

"Aye, you talk funny, aye," he said, nodding his head with a smirk, nodding toward the wave of laughter from the other half of the table. I was about to say how he talked like a hick, but Miranda caught my eye with a smile that reminded me why I was there.

I guess Brice put it together when he saw Jaylen smiling at Megan, because he shifted his focus. "So Megan," he said, leaning back in his chair, but before he had a chance to really embarrass her, a hand fell on his shoulder and his chair smacked down with a clunk. We all looked up to find Principal Sanchez.

"Mr. Wilkes, I'd rather you not lean back in your chair. We're going to need you on the football field this weekend."

"Yes, sir, sorry Mr. Sanchez," Brice said in his pretty-boy football player voice. I tried not to laugh but choked on my milk. Mr. Sanchez wandered off, and Brice set his stare on me. I wiped my nose and stared back.

"So Jack, you play sports?"

"Hockey," I said. Brice shot a look down the table to Danny and Ryan.

"Hockey?" he repeated, looking around. "You don't play football or baseball or anything?"

I think he was so used to being a jerk right to people's faces he didn't even try to hide it. But I'd had way too much of Brice Wilkes already. He waited for an answer. I glanced again at Miranda, whose "play nice" smile was the only thing keeping me in check.

"Nope, just hockey."

"That's too bad. We could use you on the football team," he

said, which might sound like a compliment, but trust me, it wasn't.

"Tragic." I took a bite of my lasagna. Megan snorted and Brice turned to her then back to me, about to make things worse between us when Miranda cut the tension, clearing her throat.

"So Jaylen, you know Megan, right?"

The faces shifted to Jaylen, who started twisting away at his braids. "Uh, yeah," he said, peeking over at Megan.

Megan jabbed her fork in his direction. "We had Mr. Turns last year, right?"

Jaylen smiled. "Yeah."

Poor Brice couldn't let go of the spotlight. He looked me over once again. "So, Miranda says you play the drums?"

I set my fork down dramatically. "Is this like, a job interview or something?"

The whole table lost it then, cracking up with laughter. Even Danny and Ryan managed a chuckle, and Brice's face matched the apple he'd been tossing in the air like a baseball. Miranda covered her mouth, a smirk peeking out from her hands.

Brice sipped his soda. "Naw man, I was just trying to get to know you. I've never met a real live Canadian before."

Before I could properly insult him, Megan cut in. "Well you *may* want to interview them. Aren't you guys starting a band?"

Everyone leaned forward. I silently cursed my new friend under my breath. The gossip moved fast around here. I swallowed hard, Miranda looked at me as though waiting for my answer. "Well, we're just going to jam, I don't know if—"

Brice smacked the table, his smirk restored. "Dude, a band? Seriously. What are you going to play?" the whole table waited for an answer.

"I don't know yet, maybe some—"

Brice's eyes lit up. "Dude, that's hilarious. I play the kazoo, and Danny can rap."

He pointed to Danny, who on cue started in with some awful beat boxing. I scanned the cafeteria for Mr. Sanchez, because I was only seconds away from removing the grin from Brice's face when Miranda tilted her head toward him.

"Why is it funny?" she asked. Danny stopped spitting into his hands. The whole table paused. Brice backed off, his cocky grin fleeing.

"No, I just mean, you know, *a band?*" He looked around for support.

"*Yes*, a band. And I'm in it too, right Jack?" Miranda said, crossing her arms. The faces bounced back to me. All I could do was nod.

"So there. We're in a band," she said, just as the bell rang. I looked at Jaylen who just nodded his head.

Great.

CHAPTER 17

Miranda dropped by the house the next day looking for her headphones. We hung out for a while on the porch, talking school, mostly. I kept her entertained with my best Brice impressions.

After a while, we fell into the Adirondack chairs, sipping Sprite, neither of us saying much. It was quiet without Trevor's constant questions and buzzing around. Only the wind whipping the clouds across the sky. I thought it might storm again.

"I'm actually surprised you and Brice don't get along better," Miranda said out of the blue.

I gasped mockingly. "What, don't we? I love Brice!"

She ignored my humor. "Because you two are kind of alike."

I dropped my act and looked at her to see if she was joking. "I'm *nothing* like that dude."

She fiddled with her bracelets (she wore like ten of them on each wrist—braided ones, rubber ones, frayed ones). "I'm not saying you guys are exactly the same, but weren't you the big hockey star up north, with like, your own little group?"

"I played hockey, yeah, but I wasn't..." I couldn't even finish my thought. I fell back into the chair. How could Miranda think I was anything like Brice? I stared across the street at nothing. Miranda giggled, leering at me cross-eyed, poking her tongue out until I had to look at her. I held tight to my scowl, but she kept on until I broke.

"You're so weird," I said, unable to stop a smile from spreading.

"Yeah, but at least I'm not pouting."

"Okay, okay. But I'm not like Brice. At all."

"Nope, not at all," she said, gazing out to the street. I huffed again just as the drizzle began. I was thinking how I wanted to read more of Dad's journals before he got home when I just sort of came out and told Miranda about it.

It. As in the journals, the sneaking around, the entries about Mom. Even as I told her, I couldn't believe I was saying it out loud. I guess I had to tell someone, it was driving me crazy.

Miranda was a great listener. She fixed her bracelets again before she looked over to me. "So you guys don't talk about her? Like, at all?"

"Nope."

"Hmm. But you want to know about your mom, right?"

"Yeah, I mean...it's weird." I shook my head. More silence. The willow tree rustled in the wind. Miranda turned to me.

"Can I see them, or..."

One minute later I was back on the porch with two of Dad's notebooks. Miranda read while I watched her take it in. How her brow scrunched with pity as she read her favorite parts out loud.

"This is so sweet. Listen to this part," she said. Then, this girl I'd just met a few weeks ago, read my dad's words.

I remember the day Jackson was born. You'd been in labor for over twenty hours and we were both beyond exhausted. I had been a mess, pacing for miles in circles during all of the tests, and dilating. But you were just as calm and cool as you always were. Ever the rock, your face was pale and your hair was a nest of sweat and tangles. When he finally came along, screaming and shaking, you held our son in your arms and it was the most natural thing I've ever seen. I was overwhelmed, scared, and tired, but you looked up to me and said, "Look what we did."

I couldn't have loved you more that day.

When she looked up her eyes were shiny. She gushed a little and I was lost, just floating through the moment with her.

"I can't believe you two never talk about this." She tapped the notebook. "I mean, this is like the sweetest thing I've ever read." She wiped her eyes with a laugh.

"I had no idea about any of this until we moved down here. It was just... She was gone and that was all."

Miranda clutched the notebook. "This is like a story book, it's so romantic. All my parents talk about are bills or summer camps, or even worse, the office."

"Okay, it's a little mushy, but it's not roman, um, romantic."

"Yes it is. It's so sweet."

I was too busy watching her when she looked up suddenly. Her smile dropped as I turned and found Dad's car rolling down the street, the music loud, thumping through the speakers.

Miranda slapped the notebook shut I snatched them from her and sat on them. There was no time to do anything else.

Dad waved at us as he got out of the car. He grabbed his laptop bag, the wind tossing his hair around. "Hey, you guys enjoying the day?"

Miranda snapped out of it first. "Homework. I was helping Jack with Algebra."

"Yeah?" Dad shot me a look. Probably because I was still in my seat hiding the evidence when usually I couldn't sit still. Well, that and Miranda was the worst actor of all times.

"Oh, okay, well, do uh, Jack I was going to see if you wanted to go try that Mexican place up the street for dinner?"

"Okay. Yeah, sure."

Miranda stood. "Well, I'll see you later."

And she was gone. And I stayed in my seat, feeling like a dirty gym towel. Dad trusted me, and I rummaged through his room. Let Miranda read his journals. What could I have been thinking?

Dad put a hand on my head. "So, Mexican?"

"Sure."

He eyed me sitting there, still. "Like, tonight?"

"Yeah," I said without budging.

"Okay." He did the whistle thing. "I'll go change." He got to the door and looked back at me once again. I smiled.

Maybe Miranda wasn't the worst actor after all.

CHAPTER 18

On Saturday afternoon, Jaylen came over for our first official jam session. I rushed out to help as he lugged his bass out of the backseat. I grabbed his amp while Dad and Mrs. Carter did the parent thing. Jaylen waved to his mom, and we shuffled down the stairs to the basement, where he handed me a handwritten list.

"So check it out, I was thinking of some songs we could start out with."

I stopped at the first song. "James Brown? I can't play James Brown."

Jaylen grinned. "Sure you can. Look man, most bands play the same old cover songs. I thought we'd funk things up some."

I wasn't sure what Jaylen was thinking with that set list. We got things hooked up, and Jaylen was going on about JB when the basement door opened and Dad came rushing down the steps.

"So Jaylen, your mother tells me your dad did some studio work."

"Yeah, he doesn't play anymore," Jaylen said, opening the case and hoisting up a shiny black bass guitar nearly as tall as he was. His voice strained under the weight of the instrument. "But he gave me this."

Dad whistled while I gawked. "Very nice. So it looks like we've got a band," Dad said.

"We're not a band," I reminded them, because no one else

would acknowledge it. Jaylen pulled out the crumpled flyer, and I couldn't stop my eyes from rolling.

"Mr. Dufresne, check this out," Jaylen said, handing Dad the tattered sheet of paper.

"Fall Bash?" Dad actually sounded interested. Jaylen strapped on the sleek bass guitar and fiddled with the amp. Dad got his guitar, and I took a seat behind the drums, shaking my head at all the band business.

"Who's going to sing?" I asked, because we would need a singer. I thought about what Miranda said at lunch.

Jaylen must have been thinking it too, because he smiled. "You know who."

"I think we *all* know who should sing," Dad said. "But let's just slow down here and see what we've got, okay?"

Jaylen slapped out a few chords, walking the bass line up the neck of the guitar. Dad's face lit up. "Maybe we've got something here," he said. "Ready Jaylen? Here we go."

Dad eased into a jam, taking it easy with the basic stuff. Jaylen smirked at the test, plucking right in behind him, head bobbing and eyes bright. Dad winked at me. Jaylen was good, and when Dad kicked into something a little faster, he just kept nodding. Fine. I started in with the beat, surprised with what we had going. It really wasn't bad.

"That's it, Jaylen," Dad yelled, his head bobbing, biting his lip, a sure sign he was feeling it.

We drifted around, changing things up halfway through songs, fast then slow, light to heavy at times. Jaylen's fingers danced on the frets, and he even plucked out a nice little bass solo. He was right about *funking* things up. It was clear Jaylen had played more than a little James Brown.

About twenty minutes in, Dad stopped playing, tilted his head, and then ran upstairs. He returned with the iPad, and I could tell by the look in his eyes we were going to be jamming for a while.

"So your dad taught you to play like that?" I asked Jaylen as he adjusted his strings.

"Yeah, he was pretty serious, at least before I was born. They did studio sessions for commercials, even some singers."

"Like, a *real* band?" I asked.

He nodded without looking up.

"Okay," Dad said excitedly, after finding whatever he was looking for. He turned the iPad around to reveal sheet music for *I Feel Good*. "I think we can play this one. Jaylen, what do you think?"

Without even glancing at the screen Jaylen cranked out the bass chord. Dad's face lit up. "Okay, no problems there. Now Jack." Dad turned to me, his hair tousled and his fingers snapping. I hadn't seen him this worked up in a while. "This is a little different than what we're used to. But you'll pick it up."

Before I could protest he scooped up the guitar. He was all over the place, hopping up and ducking his head through the strap. "Okay, guys, let's get it."

Dad and Jaylen bopped along. I had no idea where to come in, watching Dad as he jerked the neck of the guitar back, his mouth tight with concentration as he launched into a solo. It's when I knew we had something, it's when I knew for sure we were going to enter the Fall Bash.

I don't think they even noticed when I stood, slipped past them, and hit the stairs. They kept playing, Jaylen nodding and Dad kicking. I snuck out on the porch and punched Miranda's name on my phone before I lost the nerve.

"Hey."

"Hi, Jack. What's up?"

"Not much, are you busy?" I asked, trying to control the excitement in my voice.

"Umm, no, not really, just watching Trinkets. Seriously, what's up? You sound weird."

"What? No, I uh..."

She let out a gasp. "Oh my gosh. Did you talk to your dad? About, you know?"

"No. I um..." I had a feeling I was going to regret telling her about that. "We're in the basement, playing... Jaylen is here, and I was wondering if you could come. We uh, we kind of need a singer."

Some rustling on her end. "I'm sorry, a what?"

"A singer, for the band. We need you."

"You're kidding, right?"

"Hey, you said you were in. Remember, at lunch?"

"Okay, okay, I didn't know we were serious."

"Well, here's the thing. Jaylen is really good. But nobody wants to sing."

"What if I don't want to sing?"

"Um, hello. You were born to sing."

Silence on the other end, leaving my cheesy statement hanging in the air. My face went hot. Under my feet, a bass line rumbled. Dad clapping along. Finally, Miranda cleared her throat.

"Okay, give me a few minutes. And you know Trevor's going to want to come, right?"

"I figured. Just come on in, you'll hear us," I said.

"Okay, see you in a few."

I rushed back downstairs. They'd stopped playing and Jaylen sat next to Dad, the bass on his lap, watching a video. They both spun around.

"The funky drummer." Dad waved me over to where they were hovering over the iPad, watching another James Brown video. I wedged between them. About ten seconds in, I knew we had a major problem.

"I can't play that."

Jaylen nudged me. "Dude, you can, just start slow. That's what my dad says."

I fell behind my set and reluctantly picked up the sticks. I took a breath and proceeded to fumbled trough the beat. It was bad. Even with Dad and Jaylen encouraging me, the beat felt awkward and strange, stopping and starting with a slight hesitation.

Dad fiddled with some cords, hooking the iPad up to the speakers. He pressed play and we sat back and listened. I tried to focus on the beat, going through the motions. But it was useless. It was like relearning everything. "I'm serious. I can't play that."

And worse still was how Miranda was on the way and she would see me make a complete fool of myself. Move over Trevor, I was now the weak link in the chain.

"Come on, Jack, hop back there and give it a shot. Remember when you took your first lesson, how frustrated you got? That's why we practice." I waited for Jaylen to snort at my dad's little cornball pep talk, but he didn't. He was nodding.

After the video we cranked it up again. This time I took it slow. It was still terrible, but lucky for me I was with the two most optimistic people I knew. Jaylen never got frustrated, even when we kept starting over. And after a while it wasn't so bad. Far from perfect, but behind the bass and guitar it got us through.

We got back to the basics. We played I Feel Good something like twenty times. By the twenty-first time it was nearly a song. And lucky for me our singer was late, so things were almost going okay by the time Miranda hopped down the last step and took in the scene, her eyes wide in amazement.

"James Brown?" She cocked an eyebrow. Trevor knocked by

her, his trumpet in hand. Dad looked at me and then at the trumpet, his lips curling into a devilish grin.

"Oh, this is gonna be good."

"So we're gonna be a band?" Trevor asked.

Jaylen nodded. "Oh yeah."

CHAPTER 19

Jaylen and Dad went over things with Trevor. After several playful eye rolls, Miranda studied the lyrics on the iPad, and Trevor put the trumpet to his lips and produced what sounded like honking geese. He took a breath, cleared his throat, and tried again. Better. Miranda lowered the mic and looked back at me with a smile, giving me a surge of confidence.

Again, Dad's jaw went slack when Miranda belted out the lyrics, but unlike the other night, she was all business. She hit the notes so on key it was remarkable. Jaylen and I exchanged looks while Trevor remained in his own little world. We nearly made it halfway through the song on the first go around. And when the song crashed and burned, Dad looked over at Miranda.

"Holy ship prices, girl."

Miranda blushed, closing her eyes. The rest of us just stared at her because we all knew one thing. No matter how bad we played, all eyes would be on her. Ears too. I could be back there banging on pots and pans and it wouldn't make a difference. Then Dad looked over to Trevor, who took a hit of his inhaler. "And Trevor, whoa little man! Way to go!"

"Man, we've got a band," Jaylen said. I wanted to argue, but the words never made it out. Dad nodded, fiddled with a knob on his guitar, then looked us over.

"All right, guys, one more time."

And we did it again and again. My dad must have said "one more time" thirty times. Even so, my face hurt from laughing and smiling the whole time, watching Miranda snap and bob and shuffle her feet. And when she opened her mouth, it was magic.

At some time after eight, Miranda checked her phone and announced she and Trevor had to get home. We decided to practice Wednesday and Saturday nights, although I planned on hitting the drums every single day until I got that groove.

Jaylen and I walked Miranda and Trevor home. Trevor bounced around, buzzing from the music still ringing in our ears. A crescent moon smile glowing on his face.

"You're really good on that trumpet, T," Jaylen said.

"Yeah, you were good, Trevvy," Miranda said as we arrived at the Walkers' porch. Wally started barking.

Mr. Walker came to the door. "Hey guys, so what's this I hear about a band?"

Before Jaylen or I could answer, Trevor launched into every detail of practice. Miranda cut her eyes to me and shook her head. Mr. Walker nodded and then looked to us.

"James Brown, huh? I'm impressed."

"Don't be yet, we've got work to do. Well, I do at least," I said, trying to ground expectations. Not an easy feat with Trevor around. Miranda laughed, nudging my arm as she walked inside.

"You'll be fine."

Jaylen and I waved goodbye and then hiked up the dark driveway. I could almost hear Jaylen grinning.

"So does your dad still play?" I asked.

Jaylen's smile dropped and he shook his head. "Nah, not since he came home."

"Came home?"

He snickered, shaking his head at me. "Iraq, not jail."

"That's not what I meant."

"It's just fun messing with you," he said, taking a breath.

Just as quickly his smile faded. "But yeah, he got hurt pretty bad over there. Lost his legs when they hit an IED."

My steps slowed. "What?"

He twisted a braid, staring at the street before looking at me. "Like a land mine. Dad doesn't talk about it so I don't know too much. All I know is he came back and his legs were gone. And in a way, he was too."

I reminded myself to walk, searching for words. Jaylen put his hands in his pockets as we approached my house. "My dad used to be really fun. Kind of like your dad. He laughed all the time and told jokes and he used to hoist me up on his shoulders. He was so strong. But since he's been home, he's different. Way different."

"And that's why you want to do the Fall Bash so bad, right?"

He nodded. "Yep, I want to raise money for the Wounded Warrior charity. If it's cool with ya'll."

"Of course. Yeah, that sounds great."

"So we're going to do it?"

"Yeah man. Let's do it."

"Cool."

We stood at the porch, silent in our thoughts for a moment. I thought about how both of our dads were wounded in different ways. Jaylen looked over at me, his smile returning as he gave me a playful shove.

"So, you and Miranda, huh?"

I stumbled down a step. "What? Uh, why...?"

Jaylen laughed. "Bro. It's kind of obvious. But what's up with Megan?"

"Huh?" I said trying to shift gears. "Oh, uh, she thinks you're cute, and I think the band thing helps."

"Yeah, chicks dig guys in bands."

"Especially drummers."

"In that case, let's go practice some more. You need it."

We returned to the basement, where, with Jaylen's help, I was able to get the timing to a respectable pace. We kept at it until Dad called us up at ten. He'd set up the air mattress in my room, and he returned with blankets and an extra pillow. I turned on the PlayStation and asked Dad for sure about the Fall Bash. He was up for it, with, of course, some stipulations.

"Okay, so Jack, here's the deal," Dad said, tossing the pillow to Jaylen. "Your grades have to stay up. Any C's and the Fall Bash is off, okay?"

I looked to Jaylen, who nodded with a grin. Then back to Dad. "Yeah Dad, sure," I said, tossing a controller to Jaylen. The screen lit up and confusion spread across his face.

"Hockey? Come on, man."

"Sorry dude. It's the only game I own."

CHAPTER 20

Jaylen and I returned to our normal lunch table. What happened next was anything but ordinary. We were talking music when, with a drift of vanilla, Miranda plopped down beside me.

"Hey dorks."

Even as the new guy, I'd caught on quickly how things worked at Claremont. Table swapping was sort of a big deal—that much was clear when Jaylen and I made our move last week. A quick peek over to her old table. Yep, Brice had noticed.

"So, are we really doing this fund raiser thingy?" Miranda asked, digging into her lunch bag.

"Yep. Right, Jack?" Jaylen's face looked like Christmas morning with Megan sitting next to him, beaming a metallic smile.

"Seriously, in front of like, thousands of people?" Miranda persisted, but Jaylen was already unzipping his backpack.

Jaylen dug through his pack. "I hope it's thousands, more money to raise. Here, I've already got the pledge forms. Somewhere."

"Don't tell me you're shy," I said, staring at Miranda when I received a kick to my leg under the table. Miranda winked at me.

"Do I look like the shy type?"

"Tell him what you told me, then," Megan said with a giggle, and Miranda blushed. I looked from one to the other as they had an entire conversation with their eyes. Miranda smirked at me.

"Don't listen to her," she said, brushing Megan off. More giggling.

"Okay," I said, searching their faces before moving on. "Wednesday practice still work for everyone?"

Miranda nodded. "I don't have much of a choice, it's all Trevor is talking about. Did you know he's wearing a fedora now?"

I laughed, stealing another glance at Brice, who looked away as Danny blew up his paper lunch bag and smacked it with his hand so it popped like a balloon. Mr. Sanchez hustled to the scene. "Like one of those...?" I traced around my head with a finger.

"Yep, we've created some sort of hipster jazz monster."

"Sweet, I like his enthusiasm." Jaylen smiled at Megan and now *she* was blushing. Oh boy.

We discussed our set list. James Brown's "I Feel Good" made the cut, but we needed a few more songs. Megan mentioned a string of poppy tunes that didn't fit our style, and I'd never get my dad on board with playing a Katy Perry song.

While we argued over music, I kept checking Miranda's old table, watching Brice. I wasn't sure if Miranda's departure was temporary, Miranda never came out and said anything about it. But it seemed to me whatever was or wasn't going on between her and the quarterback, she seemed to be over. And when she looked up to me with that smile, I liked this band thing more and more.

THIS BAND THING WAS A DISASTER. Nothing went right on Wednesday. Dad was late because of some stupid deadline at work. Then he broke a string. Miranda's phone beeped and buzzed nonstop, and I kept fumbling the beat. Trevor—who was in fact wearing a fedora— forgot his inhaler. Only Jaylen seemed okay, and I felt bad he had to be there for our falling apart.

Even Miranda's singing couldn't save us. We changed things up, simplifying the songs, but we couldn't even get "Louie Louie" down. It was brutal.

After an hour or so, when it was obvious things weren't getting anywhere, Miranda and Trevor escaped, begging off to go eat dinner. Jaylen called his mom. Dad went upstairs. That left me. The lonely drummer.

I watched YouTube videos of James Brown. His drummer was a man named Clyde Stubblefield, AKA, the funky drummer. His sound was impossible for me to duplicate. I went through the motions again and again, determined to get it right. But something just wasn't clicking.

I sat on my stool, staring at the Jimi Hendrix poster I'd hung crookedly on the cinder block walls when we first moved in. I had to admit I was having a lot more fun this year than I thought possible. The whole band idea had taken my mind off of Plattsburgh and what I'd left behind. Jaylen was cool, and Miranda, was, well, confusing, but in a good way. I could deal with Brice. The only thing I couldn't get off my mind was the thing with Dad.

When I got upstairs Dad was talking to Grandpa. He waved me over and passed the phone, and I smiled when I heard his familiar gravelly voice and North Country accent.

"How are the Rangers doing?" I asked.

He sighed into the phone. "Not too hot, bunch of knuckleheads this year."

We talked about the local teams. How it had already snowed up at Saranac Lake. Grandpa was packing up for one of his trips to the camp, where he hung with the other old farts as they pretended to hunt. Dad and I both knew he never took a shot.

"Did Dad tell you we formed a band?"

"Warned a man?" Grandpa said, and I smiled. I figured he didn't have his hearing aide in.

"WE FORMED A BAND," I yelled. "We're gonna enter the Fall Bash next month."

"Oh? Well, I hope you found a singer. That father of yours is a great guitar player, but he can't sing a lick. Sounds like a wounded coyote giving birth to—"

"Grandpa, we've got a singer. Her name is Miranda. She lives down the street. You should hear her sing."

"So you've met a girl?" he said, his voice a little higher.

"Well, no, I just, she's..." My brain locked up and Grandpa laughed.

"Ah yes, you've met a girl, all right."

Funny how he could hear *some* things, I thought. I imagined Grandpa sitting by his bay window, watching war movies and nodding off. Later that evening he'd go to the school where he worked the scorer's table at the hockey games. He said he'd visit soon, but I didn't push. Grandpa was a man of routine, I guess we all are.

But routines change.

CHAPTER 21

Not all routines change. Right after school the next day I snuck back into Dad's room.

Lately I've been thinking about prom, when I was a senior with one foot out the door, ready to go off to school. I was counting the days until I could get out of Plattsburgh and never come back.

Jessica Tillman. Ha, remember? She was cute in her own way. But just think, if she hadn't come down with the flu and cancelled on me hours before the dance, I would have been there stepping on her toes instead of picking up my little sister and her friends.

When Mom asked me to pick you guys up, I felt so lame. At least until I pulled into the parking lot outside the gym. You were sitting on the curb nearly in tears. Wow, you were beautiful. Your hair was pinned up and curled. Your dress still perfect. When Genna told me what happened, I parked the car and hauled your drunken prom date into the back seat. To this day I can still smell his whisky breath on my face.

My heart jumped when you climbed up front with me, wiping your eyes, trying to put on a smile.

I'd already pieced together that Dad was kind of dorky and shy. I smiled reading about how Mom was Aunt Genna's pretty and popular friend and how Dad was crushing on her. And it read like after prom the feeling was mutual. I leaned back, listening for any sounds of a car pulling up or steps on the front porch. Then it was back to the pages.

That whole summer was a blur, while I was preparing to go to school and you still had a couple of years left back in town. Genna was mad at first, but over time she realized it wasn't a fling. Our daily picnics at the park, the hikes at the point. With you, Plattsburgh was a brand-new place. Summer whirled by and Dad basically had to drag me to Clarkston. I was all but ready to drop out.

Thankfully I could come home every weekend. And you even came up a few times until your parents got suspicious. We'd count down the days until Winter Break, Spring Break, summer, and the time together flew by. And then came the talk with your father, just after I finished my freshman year and you were heading into your senior year.

I wiped the Cheetos' dust on my shorts then stuffed the notebook back in its place. In the kitchen, I cracked open a Sprite and mixed it with an orange Gatorade, thinking about the journals. I couldn't stay away from them now. I'd gotten through maybe ten notebooks, and there were many more to go. But each one I read only made it harder to hide my betrayal from Dad.

On Friday, Miranda, Trevor, and I were banging around in the basement when we heard a stampede above our heads. Dad's work buddies. I tossed my sticks and we scrambled upstairs only to find a nerd-fest in full swing on the back deck.

"Jack!" Dad called, and I stepped outside where there were two old guys, two younger guys, and one girl. Dad went through the introductions, and I nodded and tried to catch their names.

The girl's name was Vicki, the guy with the beard was Jeff, there was a Paul, and a Rick who smoked cigarettes and rolled with laughter at anything you said. I forgot the last guy's name, but he didn't really say too much.

Vicki looked about my dad's age, maybe younger, with short jagged hair and friendly eyes. She seemed to be holding her own with the guys as they talked about deadlines and projects and other boring adult work stuff, and it wasn't long before Miranda made faces in the window, causing me to burst out laughing. Dad gave me a funny look, and I told him we'd be in the basement.

"Tell Miranda if she keeps crossing her eyes like that they may stay that way," Dad said, grinning.

I rushed inside, Miranda was still peeking out from the kitchen with a smirk while Trevor helped himself to a soda in the fridge.

"You got so busted," I said, but Miranda wasn't paying attention.

"That Vicki girl is pretty," she said, her now straight eyes full of thought. "You think she and your dad—"

I covered my ears. "Nope, not listening."

"Gross," Trevor yelled.

I shook my head and dragged the two of them back to the basement where I banged out a drum solo to drown out Miranda's teasing. We liked to play this game where I'd hit the pop snare drum and Miranda tried not to blink. I loved watching her tremble and giggle in anticipation and then jump with a squeal as soon as I'd crack the drum.

Miranda picked up Dad's guitar, giving it a light strum and playfully swinging her head, singing "Love is in the Air." I banged louder and she sang louder. *Bang. Sing. Bang. Strum.* In fact, we were making so much noise we didn't see them all standing at the stairs with shocked faces as they watched. I stopped drumming, and Miranda whipped around to find them gawking.

"Whoa. That girl's got some pipes," said the Jeff guy. Rick hacked. Miranda blushed wildly, carefully setting Dad's pearl white guitar back in its stand. I'd been around it my whole life and never knew it was a 1999 Stratocaster. But now, even with the back being all scarred and scuffed from his belt buckle, I knew it was my dad's most prized possession. I'd read about how my mom had bought it for him on their first anniversary.

Dad broke the silence, stepping down and grabbing the guitar. "Grab that mic, Miranda."

Miranda hopped in place. The amp screeched with feedback as Dad made an adjustment. He looked at me and Miranda and smiled as if to say, *let's show them something*. I couldn't wait to see their reactions when they heard Miranda's voice when it really got going, and when we cranked up "Mustang Sally," five collective jaws dropped in unison.

After that, the nerds stormed the small basement room, dancing and whooping and singing along. Miranda was a natural front man, or, front *girl*, as she looked back at me and belted out the chorus. *Ride, Sally, Ride!*

Trevor jiggled the tambourine because he didn't have his trumpet. Vicki danced with him, bumping his hip until he blushed.

Later that night, the guys left but Vicki hung around for dinner. I think Miranda was right, there was something going on. I hadn't seen Dad with a girl before, and it was strange, her being in the house. My phone buzzed. It was a text message from Miranda.

Is she still there?

Yeah

Told you. ☺

CHAPTER 22

Around four Saturday evening, a Ford Windstar parked at the curb in front of the house. Jaylen hopped out and opened the side door. Inside the van, a crane-like contraption unfolded where the seat would've been, and a figure maneuvered himself into position. Dad and I stepped out onto the porch just as Jaylen hit the steps. "Hey, my dad wanted to meet you, Mr. Dufresne, if that's cool?"

"Yeah, sure. Does he need some help?" Dad said and Jaylen shrugged, looking back at the van.

"You can try, but he won't let you."

The motor cranked as an elevator lowered Mr. Carter to the street. In no time he was out, shutting the door and wheeling himself up to the porch. The first thing I noticed about Jaylen's dad, besides the fact he was in a wheel chair, was his hardened face. Maybe it was because of what Jaylen told me, but his dad's eyes looked numb, like they had seen really bad things—things that put normal life at a distance.

"How you doing?" he asked, coming up the walkway. His voice was firm and serious. Sometimes I forgot how some kids had strict dads, because it had always been Grandpa's job to scare me straight. Dad strode down the steps to meet him with a handshake.

"Mr. Carter. I'm Cliff Dufresne and this is my son Jackson."

Mr. Carter nodded at me. His hair was cropped and trimmed close on the sides. A chinstrap beard to his mustache. I tried my best not to look at the void in his lap.

"So you must be this great drummer Jaylen's told me so much about."

"Well, not *great*," I said sheepishly.

I looked to Jaylen, who laughed. "He's getting it, Dad. They play a lot of rock and stuff, so JB is a little different. But we'll get there."

Mr. Carter nodded. Dad picked up the slack. "Well, your son here plays a mean bass guitar. I hear he has you to thank for that."

"I taught him what I knew. He's taken to it and wants to put in the time, so I think he's going to be good," he said matter-of-factly.

"Are you gonna stay for practice, Mr. Carter?" I asked, but then felt really stupid because how was he going to get down there? But he gave it some thought, then looked at Jaylen.

"Well, sure, I'll see what ya'll got," he said. Just then Mr. Jacobsen's Buick slowed and then crawled into his driveway, and I thought he was going to pull a muscle the way he wrenched his neck to see what was going on in the yard. Mr. Carter eyed the side fence but Jaylen was a step ahead.

"The back door is wide enough, Dad. You can make it."

Mr. Carter took one more peek around the side of our bungalow, sizing up the hill. I could tell he wanted no favors coming his way—even though it didn't feel like a favor, helping him inside so he could help us practice. Seemed like a fair trade.

"Okay, let's do it."

Jaylen wasn't kidding; Mr. Carter asked for and needed no help. The Hawk tattoo on his forearm bulged and twitched as he guided the chair down the sloping hill, over the roots and grass and down onto the back patio without breaking a sweat. I'd never seen such strength.

The chair fit by a fraction, and after some deft maneuvering on his part, Mr. Carter was in. He and Dad talked music while

Jaylen and I set up. It wasn't long before Mr. Carter chuckled. I smiled too, because Dad may be a bigtime dork, but he sure knew how to make people feel comfortable.

We powered to life, Jaylen bounced a few chords on the bass and I tinkered with my set when the door upstairs opened and Trevor bustled down the steps. Then Miranda, Megan, Mrs. Walker, and lastly, Mr. Walker, all filed in. Mr. Walker had to duck to keep from clunking his head.

Once everyone was nice and crammed into our small basement, I stood up and smiled at Miranda. "Running a little late I see. Man, what a diva," I said, tapping my wrist. She gave a semi-serious stare, then strode up to the mic and dished out a trademark eye roll.

"Sorry, Megan took her time getting here, and then Mom and Dad decided they wanted to be entertained." Miranda looked to Mr. Carter, Jaylen cleared his throat and introduced his dad. Mr. Carter's jaw tightened, and I think he was a little uncomfortable with all the new company, but Dad was quick with the pleasantries and kept things moving along.

When we were all acquainted and seated, or just sort of standing around looking at my dirty clothes on the floor, Dad strummed a few chords. "Okay people, places."

I jumped behind my set. Megan giggled, plopping down on an old dusty ottoman that came with the house. I twirled a drumstick, ready for our maiden performance, when Megan waved her arms to get our attention.

"Hang on, what's the name of this band?" she asked, finger quoting the word band. All five of us froze. Trevor's first notes nosedived.

"We haven't gotten that far yet." He looked at me. I looked at Jaylen.

"Ideas?" Dad said, with a quick riff on the guitar. "Every band needs a name."

We sat there, each of us scrambling our brains as the amplifiers hummed along with the air conditioning.

"The Jackson Five?" Trevor offered.

A collective moan. "That's been done," Jaylen said.

"It has?" he said.

"Uh, let's see, The Five Cast?" I said, a play on Dad's old band name. Miranda tilted her head, one hand firmly on her hip.

"That doesn't make any sense."

Dad strummed another little riff, one he played from time to time while we tossed out names ranging from horrible to just plain stupid. There was a bark at the back door, breaking our collective brainstorm. Miranda looked at Trevor.

"Did you or did you not forget to put Wally inside after his walk?" Mr. Walker asked both kids. He liked to ask questions in the form of a riddle.

"I didn't walk him last," Miranda countered, then turned to Mrs. Walker. "Did you walk Wally, Mom?"

"Nope."

"Bring him in, the more the merrier," Dad said as Miranda neared the door. "Unless anyone's allergic," he said, looking around. Miranda opened the door and Wally burst inside, frantically wagging and sniffing. Trevor jumped up with his horn.

"The Wallywalkers!"

Miranda laughed. Dad nodded. I repeated it to myself. Not bad.

"The Wallywalkers. I like it," Dad said.

"Me too," Jaylen agreed, thumping his bass.

Mr. Walker shrugged. "The Wallywalkers. Perfect."

With our name settled, we got down to business. Warming up with "Louie Louie," our audience rocked and sang along.

Then we went into "Wild Thing," Miranda adlibbing silly lyrics as usual.

You would have thought Wally would have enjoyed our stuff, being the namesake of the band and all. But just like thunder, he wasn't a fan of my drums. He barked along at the cymbals, and Mr. Walker had to run him home after he scrambled onto Megan's lap.

Mr. Carter gave Jaylen a few pointers from time to time, and I hit him with a few questions of my own, the guy being a real musician and all. Then it was time for the funky stuff. Mr. Walker returned, sitting down just in time for us to hit "I Feel Good" and "Papa's Got A Brand New Bag."

We were good, not great, but I kept the beat simple and didn't try to get flashy, knowing Miranda would carry us. Her voice was like a powerful gust in our sails, setting us on course. It was our job to just try and keep up.

I'd gotten better at the little hesitation in my drumming, and Dad played the quick riffs like he'd been doing it for years. Toss in Jaylen's bass and our trumpet player and we might just fool some people into thinking we were a soul band.

Miranda danced and shuffled and did her thing. When we finished, she let go with a screech and did this crazy twirl. Megan stood up on the ottoman, and Mr. and Mrs. Walker joined the standing ovation.

"Lord have mercy, girl. You've got a voice like an angel," Mr. Carter said after clapping. Miranda blushed, still heaving from all the singing and moving.

"Thank you."

"She's like a little Aretha Franklin," he continued. I made a mental note to Google "the queen of soul." We all looked at each other, our smiles saying the same thing. We weren't half bad. Megan hopped down and stood next to Jaylen. Mr. and Mrs. Walker beamed with pride at their kids.

The music seemed to have loosened up Mr. Carter. He tilted his head and rolled his chair to my dad. "Hey Cliff, what was that little riff you were playing earlier?"

"Huh, oh just something I play around with from time to time."

"Do uh, do you mind playing it again?"

Dad looked a little flustered. "Uh, sure."

He strummed the slow, gloomy chords, but I guess like the painting, and the guitar, I'd gotten used to it over the years. But Mr. Carter's face said something different. He must have thought it was something special.

"And it's just something you came up with?"

"Yeah, nothing really."

"No, I like it. Kind of bluesy. But do me a favor, speed it up a little."

Dad cleared his throat, looked at his guitar, and then played it again, only faster. Jaylen looked at me, and Miranda smiled because it worked. It was great. Mr. Carter thought it sounded like a Van Morrison song. He nodded at Jaylen who picked up the rhythm, and before I knew it, I was tapping the snare. Mr. Carter swayed in his wheelchair, and when we saw his head nodding along, we knew the Wallywalkers had their first original song.

Now we just needed lyrics.

CHAPTER 23

Our lunch table was the hotspot of the cafeteria, with people dropping by asking questions about the band. They wanted to know what kind of music we played, where could they see us, and if we were going on tour. With Megan plugging the Wallywalkers on the morning announcements, publicity came cheap and easy. But man did the rumors swirl.

I heard you guys got a record deal!

What night are you going to be on America's Got Talent?

Are you guys playing the pep rally?

We *were* doing the pep rally. Miranda and Megan worked it out with Mrs. Newton who mentioned something to Mr. Peters, the music teacher, who brought it up with Coach Milton. Next thing I knew we were slotted to play a song through the introductions and after the rally. All of that was great, besides one glaring problem. Our forty-year-old guitarist wasn't a student.

But a pep rally wasn't exactly the Super Bowl halftime show, and like I said about Miranda's voice, we could get by banging on buckets.

Also boosting our newfound fame were the flyers Trevor had printed up about the fundraiser. He'd plastered the school and any utility pole within a two-mile radius. Oh yeah, and he'd recorded our practice and posted two songs up on YouTube—both of our James Brown covers. We were up to something like two-thousand hits. The Wallywalkers were trending.

So we had a little buzz going. But there was the whole issue with our name. When Miranda said *Wallywalkers*, she made it sound almost cool. Besides, no one was going to argue with her anyway.

Well, maybe one person.

"What kind of name is that, anyway?"

Brice sat a couple of rows behind me in the bleachers before gym class on Monday. "It sounds like something my little sister would come up with," he said, being sure I could hear. His little followers laughed, but I'd had enough. I turned right around to face him.

"How does it feel?"

"What?" he asked, looking around as if to say, *who is this crazy guy?*

"Having a little sister with a better vocabulary than you?"

Everybody got quiet. Brice opened his mouth but didn't say anything, and we sat there facing off until Mr. Hatch entered the gym, ready to test our endurance.

I could do this all day.

THAT EVENING I was with Miranda, strolling down by the camp, when she turned to me, the evening sun glittering in her green eyes. "Did you get in a lot of fights at your old school?"

"No, not really," I said. Then, after some thought. "Maybe a few on the ice, but that's hockey. Why?"

She looked off into the woods, then her brown eyes found mine. "I mean, don't get me wrong, I think you're a nice guy. But at school, you have this...hmm, how should I say it. I don't know, like this edge. You puff up and it's like you're...different."

"Different?"

"Yeah, especially when Brice is around."

I picked up a stick, dragging it in the gravel underneath the weeds and clovers. After a few steps I shrugged. "I guess…I'm new. I don't want people to think I'm soft."

Miranda's shoulders dropped a little. She was still giggling when she looked back to me. "Soft? It's school, not jail, Jack."

I dropped my smile. Miranda had a way of making me look at things differently. Maybe all girls did, but Miranda especially. At the camp, we sat together on the two four-by-fours laid across a couple of stumps to make a bench. I took a breath then pulled out a piece of paper and handed it to her.

"Well, here. Read this since you think I'm such a tough guy."

She unfolded the page—the poem Dad had written about my mom. I watched as Miranda read it, twice, and then one more time, her lips moving along with the words like she was singing it to herself. I knew what she was doing because I'd done it too. Then she turned to me.

"Jack, we should play this."

"We can't. He doesn't know I know, remember?"

Miranda dropped the paper to her lap. Like a spy, I'd snuck into Dad's room and copied it while he was on the computer working on a project. Risky move, but I couldn't get it out of my head. I'd read it over the summer, and when dad played that riff, it all came together. It fit like my own two hands clasping together.

Wally barked to get us moving. Miranda and I stood up, still studying the piece of paper. "This is it," she whispered, her eyes pleading. I knew what was coming. Maybe it's why I'd given it to her in the first place.

"Look, you're going to have to talk to him."

"I know," I said, because she was right, I did need to talk to him. I just didn't know how.

CHAPTER 24

Dad tossed in a hundred bucks and we had our first donation for the Fall Bash. Practice wise, we had our hands full, between Mr. Carter and his soul influences combined with my dad and his rock influences, we were all over the place. But Miranda's range left us with no limitations. Dad and Mr. Carter had us watching all sorts of videos—Aretha Franklin (Mr. Carter was right about Miranda sounding like her), Janis Joplin, and Pat Benatar. It was like music school.

The Wallywalkers. We had Jaylen, born and raised on funk and soul. He knew the James Brown stuff, Temptations, Otis Redding, and so on. Then there were Dad and me. We'd always played classic rock and touched on some blues. Dad loved Dylan, the Stones, and Zeppelin, but we'd noticed how a lot of it was similar, it was all about style.

Trevor was jazz and classical, but he was game for anything. Which left Miranda, who liked the pop stuff on the radio but really just loved music. I don't know how to truly describe just how good her voice was, you just had to hear it.

Still, we had problems. The main one being the third song on our set list. Everybody argued, pushing for something different, until Miranda showed Dad's poem/song or whatever it was to Jaylen and Trevor. Then it was settled, at least to them it was, especially when Miranda sang it softly in the basement.

But then came Wednesday.

While my dad was upstairs finishing up some work on the laptop, Jaylen was bugging me to talk to Dad about it. Like it was that easy. I was getting frustrated with the whole mess. I *really* regretted showing Miranda the "song" in the first place. I thought she'd understand how, for me at least, this was about a whole lot more than some dumb song.

"Dude, we *have* to play it, it's an original. Besides, it's perfect," Jaylen kept on, and I kept on ignoring him. Miranda hadn't said a word, but I already knew how she felt. Then Trevor hopped into the conversation.

"Yeah, it sounds like something on the radio."

I bashed the cymbal. "Look, I'll talk to him when I talk to him. Until then can we shut up about it?" I said, surprised at my own voice. Jaylen and Trevor exchanged looks. Miranda glared at me, her eyes pinning me to the wall.

The door opened and Dad rushed down, walking right into the storm. "Sorry, that went a little over. Okay let's... Um, what's going on?"

I tensed, ready to chuck a drumstick if Trevor started blabbing about the song. Jaylen cut a glance at Miranda, who looked at Dad and then to me blankly. "Nothing. Jack's just in a mood, that's all."

Dad turned to me. "You okay, buddy?"

"Yeah, whatever. Let's just play some music."

We tore through rehearsal. Dad's song hung over the room as we blasted through our small catalogue. Our newest addition, Aretha Franklin's "Respect" was dead on. With Miranda's showmanship to go along with the voice, it was a lock. She counted down the end of the song, and Dad gave her a dorky high-five.

When we took five, Miranda grabbed her water and looked over to my dad. "Hey, Mr. Dufresne, about that song you were playing the other night. Can we do that one again?" I glanced at Dad, a boiler ticking inside of me. The impatient buzz of the amplifier filled the room as I clenched my teeth, locking every muscle in my legs.

Dad simply nodded with a shrug. "Yeah, let's do it."

He wound the guitar into the song. I shot Miranda a cold stare as she swayed along, no doubt singing the lyrics about my mother in her head. But it was impossible to ignore how perfectly they fit together. And while Dad was lost in the chords, my drumming was too loud and clumsy for the gentle song. Not that I cared.

Miranda stepped forward, gripping the microphone. My lips tightened and my arms turned to lead. If she started belting out the song, Dad would know I'd been in his closet, reading his notebooks. He'd know I'd shared them with other people, his deepest most intimate thoughts about our life—Mom's life.

Miranda lifted her head to the mic. She took a breath and parted her lips. Just as she was about to sing my confession to the world, I smashed the cymbal and jumped up, my stool crashing to the ground, sucking the song out of the room.

"I'm not doing this." I stomped out the back door and slammed it. Outside, my face tingled, like there was a chemical reaction with my anger and the heat. I leaped over the fence, wiping my face and stalking around the house, where I fell onto the porch steps, burying my head between my knees and wishing I'd never agreed to be in a dumb band with an even dumber name.

It wasn't long before I heard Trevor's voice. I looked up. Miranda started to say something but then changed her mind. She grabbed her brother and led him home. A few moments later, Mr. Carter's van pulled up.

Dad helped with the amp, and Jaylen gave me a wave as he got in the van. I watched them pull away, leaving me alone with Dad and the big fat wedge of a secret between us.

He walked toward the porch and dropped his eyes down to me. "You want to tell me what's going on?"

Gone was the usual humor in his voice. His song still played in my head, over and over, charging the air between us. Since the very first day I'd been sneaking around. But the secrets had only filled me with anger and confusion. I knew it was time. And still I stalled. "What do you mean?"

"What do *I* mean?" He threw up his hands. "You bit everyone's head off back there. Wanna tell me why you snapped?"

"I'm fine, it's just..." I sputtered like a leaking dam. Nothing would be the same once I said it. Then again, nothing had been the same since we got here.

Dad climbed up the porch and slid into the chair. Something about the carefree way he did it stirred something up in my stomach.

"It's just what, Jack?"

The crows in Mr. Jacobsen's trees squawked, hopping from limb to limb. Wally barked in the distance. Once again I was chipping away at the old wall, on the verge but afraid of what was on the other side. All I had to do was say the words to my dad, the man who had raised me and loved me since the day I was born. And still...

"Nothing, I've just had a bad day. A real bad day."

Dad sat back. "Look, I know what you mean, and I'm so proud of you and how you've adjusted to this move. I was having second thoughts for a while, but you seem okay. Better than okay. But listen, if you still really want to go home, we can talk about it. Okay?"

What? My face flushed. My nose tingled as my body flooded with fear. The wall was collapsing. Everything was collapsing. I jumped to my feet and looked into my dad's widening eyes. "I don't want to leave, Dad. I want to talk about Mom."

No going back now. I wiped my eyes, feeling too old to cry but too helpless to stop the tears. I looked away because it was easier that way. "You always say we're a team. How we can talk about anything. But we can't. We can't talk about the biggest thing in the world to us. We can't talk about how Mom died and how you can't get over it."

He sat motionless, stuck to the chair. His mouth opened but then snapped shut. His easygoing smile, as much a part of him as his nose or ears, vanished. His eyes pooled with tears.

I started to say more, to throw it all back at him and hurt him again, but the look on his face stopped me cold. Besides, I wasn't even mad at him. I wasn't really mad at all. When I realized that, I stumbled ahead, whispering, "She was *my mom*, Dad. I want to know her. But you won't let me."

A car horn in the distance reminded me life would continue. The world would go on with or without us. I shook my head and took a few steps toward him. "I know you still talk to her, Dad, but she's gone. She's gone and I'm right here."

I hunched over. My legs couldn't hold the weight of my body. After a moment he shifted in his seat. He took my hand and squeezed it. His breaths came shaky and short and he nodded like he was agreeing with some unheard voice in his head. "Do you know how many nights I've stayed up wishing I was a better father to you? How sometimes, I wished you had her, instead..."

I shook my head again, not letting him finish. "Dad, no."

"I haven't been fair to you," he said, quietly, almost to himself. "To us." He stood up and hugged me so hard I shuddered. "It just hurts so damn much," his voice cracked— ripped and jagged. I'd never seen my dad cry before, and it only made me cry harder. He pulled back from me, and I wiped my face, unable to hold his glossy stare. "I've messed this up bad, huh kiddo?"

It threw me off, seeing him cry. While at the same time a wave of relief washed over me because it was finally out in the open—this wide gaping hole we could either try to fix or just fall into. And I think he felt the same way. At least I hoped he did.

Dad wiped his face, his breaths still quivering. "I thought I could protect you from the pain, it's... I'm sorry, Jackson."

"Dad, I don't need to be protected. I just need... I just need you."

We both wiped our eyes, stared down at our feet. Dad nodded again and again. He wiped his face. "Oh man. I used to talk to Grandpa about this. He kept telling me just to talk to you about her, and I kept saying you weren't ready. But it was me. I wasn't ready. Then the years just...passed."

Fresh tears rolled down my face, but they were good tears. It was already getting easier. We fell into our chairs as a gentle breeze swept over us, watching the falling leaves dance down the street like skeletons of summer. The wall was down and that was a start.

And then I remembered I still had more to say. "Dad, there's something else," I said, wanting to lay it all out there on the porch. "When we moved, I found your... I found your journals."

His eyes cut to me and I watched him take it in. How I'd pried my way into his secret thoughts. He pulled his hair back and I caught a flash of a few gray strands I hadn't noticed before. "You read them?" His chest deflated as he exhaled, as though he'd been holding his breath for years and could finally breathe. Then he started again, this time his voice was lower. "Jack, look—"

"I'm sorry dad, I feel bad, but it's the only way I could learn about her. I've been sneaking in and reading."

He shook his head. "No, Jack it's...oh boy. It's okay, it's fine.

I mean, I just—I never thought you wanted to talk about her. I just never knew when we'd be ready. Does that make sense?"

"I guess. But I do need to talk about her. I *want* to talk about her," I said, and he closed his eyes. I leaned closer. "Dad. Are you okay? I mean some of the stuff in there, it's sad."

He stared off at something across the street—a tree or a bird, or maybe nothing at all. Another wave of tears crashed, and he wiped his eyes. "A lot of it, Jack, it just helped me cope. I thought it would get easier, and it has...most of it has. But for a while, it was just getting those feelings out on the page. And after she was gone, it helped me. It felt like I was writing to her, like she was still here. In the other room or at the grocery store. Sounds crazy, huh?"

I wiped my hands on my legs, nodding, shrugging, nodding again. "No. Yeah. I don't know."

My arms and legs were heavy, like I'd played in a hockey tournament. "Dad, I've realized how special she was. But...to me, *you're* that special."

He turned to me then, smiling through the tears. "Thanks, Jack. You're an amazing kid, you know?" His voice trailed. "Man, I've really bungled this whole thing up," he gushed, pulling his hair back. I'd never seen him look so confused. So vulnerable.

"No, Dad, you haven't. I couldn't ask for a better dad. Trust me, I would have never moved down here for anyone else."

"Thanks, Jack," he said, a little smile parting his lips. We sat like that for a minute, listening to the birds, watching the leaves, our hands wet with tears and the silence healing our wounds. Then, without warning, Dad just opened the vault.

"The way she used to look at you. It was...she was such a great mother. She could always soothe you when you were upset. You would always call for her first, too. I was like chopped liver or something."

"Really?"

"Oh yeah," he said, the smile widening. "I didn't stand a chance. You were a mama's boy through and through."

And then he gave me the best gift he'd ever given me, bits and pieces of my mother. The sound of her voice, how she could always calm him when he was upset. Her smile. And the strange thing was how it wasn't even weird, it was the most natural thing in the world. He even talked about her flaws like they were what made her so special to him. He said she had no idea how to do laundry or how to work the vacuum.

"Even I know how to vacuum, Dad. You're such a sucker," I said, and it wasn't long before we were out there laughing, our faces still red and puffy and wrinkled from the sudden change of gears. Dad looked over at me with a blubbery smile.

"There's so much of her in you. I see it every day. And the scary part is, it's not how you look just like her, you even have the same gestures and mannerisms."

"Really?"

He let out a sniffling laugh, mimicking me. "Oh yeah, like this thing? How you talk with your hands when you're excited? All her."

Pretty soon we were whooping it up. If Mr. J was looking out his bay window, he must have thought we were a couple of kooks out there. Dad tapped me on the head and went in to grab a couple sodas. When he returned he had one of the notebooks.

"I'm glad you went snooping through my stuff," he said. "But you know what? I would have been on to you sooner or later."

"Really," I said as he handed me a Sprite. "How's that?"

He flipped the notebook toward me, and I saw the undeniable smudges of bright orange Cheetos stains.

"Oh, sorry."

"No big deal." He took his seat. "It goes with all my stains," he said, his voice easy again. He rifled through the notebook, looking for something he wanted to show me about Mom. "Oh, here it is."

I sat back and Dad read to me from his journal. And through his words and his voice, Mom came alive, right there on the porch of our house, somewhere in the sunset of Virginia

CHAPTER 25

On Thursday, Mr. Carter arrived early to pick me up for school. Jaylen and I loaded up the van, then unloaded the van. I spent seventh period setting up for the pep rally as the gym class looked on. Brice stood to the side, his arms crossed over his football jersey like a tool, as he tried not to stare.

Jaylen shot me a grin, then turned to his bass as I set up the mic for Miranda, who abandoned a group of whispering girls to assist us with the final touches. We'd all made up after my outburst at practice, at least after I'd begged everyone's forgiveness right before I told them how Dad and I had finally had a talk. Like, *The talk.* After that, Miranda fell into me for a hug, and I'd been flying high ever since.

Miranda plugged up the mic and checked it a few times. By the time Mr. Hatch arrived, gym was forgotten as everyone was asking us to play a song. I inspected my kit closely, I'd worried most of the day about my poor drums, sitting in the gym, inviting any idiot to start banging away.

Now there was a crowd. And Brice came strutting over with his meatheads, his cocky smile on full tilt. "All right, we've got a big-time band here, let's hear a little sneak peek."

"We're playing the pep rally," Miranda said flatly. I think she was finally getting tired of Brice's routine, too.

"Come on, just give us a little preview," he said, looking around. "Let's hear the great Wallywackers."

I whipped around, slinging the mic cord to the floor. But Miranda shook her hair from her face, shot Brice a look, and with her best innocent girl impression, turned to the coach. "Mr. Hatch, do you mind if we do a sound check for the pep rally?"

Mr. Hatch glanced around the gym, mulling it over. It was all Miranda needed as she waltzed over and grabbed the microphone. She shot a smile to Jaylen and me. We looked at each other, shrugged, then followed her to our setup.

"Uh, sure. Okay. I guess." Mr. Hatch shrugged, looking to the main doors. And right then, gym class turned into absolute chaos. With no lead guitar, Jaylen began walking the bass line, *bump ba bump ba bump ba bump.* I fell behind my set. Miranda unclasped the microphone, cleared her throat, and launched into "Some Kind of Wonderful."

She started slow, almost shy by her standards, getting a feel for the acoustics of the gymnasium. I kept the beat, waiting, knowing what was coming. And when Miranda closed her eyes and hit the chorus, her voice boomed off the walls and filled every crevice to the rafters.

Faces lit up, and soon after that kids started dancing and screaming, cheering us on. Well, most of the kids, Brice drifted back to the bleachers, arms crossed over his chest, still careful not to wrinkle his precious jersey.

Heads popped in from the hallways and more bodies filtered into the gym. And with them came Vice Principal Newton, threading her way through the crowd while waving her arms and motioning for us to drop it. The bass line drooped to a halt.

"Whoa, um excuse me," she said, looking around. "We're not quite ready. The pep rally starts at two forty-five." She checked the clock and then looked over to Miranda, breaking out of her teacher voice. "Wow, that was... I could hear you guys from my office."

"Sorry, we were just rehearsing for the pep rally."

Mrs. Newton smiled incredulously. "Well, I think you've

got it."

The warmup relaxed us, and soon after the final bell the bleachers filled and an excited murmur hit the gym. Jaylen and Miranda looked around just as Trevor hustled over wearing his little hat and with his trumpet case swinging at his side. "Hey, I didn't know we were doing a sound check!"

"Neither did we," Jaylen said. Trevor dropped to a knee, unbuckling his case and pulling out his shiny trumpet. He stood and looked around dramatically.

"Well, this is it, Wallywalkers. Our first gig!"

The gym was stifling hot as the entire student body crammed in. Mrs. Newton strode out purposely to the microphone. We sat on the front row of the bleachers. After some well-dressed threats about behavior and conduct, she handed the mic over to Coach Milton, who wasted no time. He shook his fist and screamed, "Welcome, Rhinos!"

I jumped and Miranda laughed. The bleachers thundered, and he motioned a hand to his ear. "I can't hear you! I said *Welcome*, Rhinos!"

The football coach, Coach Milton, puffed his chest and adjusted his hat before gearing up with his coach speak. *Great team this year...gonna be a dogfight out there... Need your support...*

The response was deafening, any excuse to stomp the bleachers and whoop and cheer and whistle. You would have thought we were heading to the Super Bowl. I looked at my bandmates, all smiles. Trevor, the sixth grader, was on top of the world.

Coach Milton's face went a ruddy red as he rumbled through the end, finishing with a hearty *Go Rhinos* before nodding to us. We took our places and Jaylen cranked up the bass line.

"All right, now let's introduce our team."

I crashed the cymbals as Coach Milton went through the lineup. Brice ran out like he was on the Teen Choice Awards, full speed, red-faced, pumping his fist. Coach Milton smiled at his star as Brice cranked up that fake smile of his, motioning for the bleachers to stand before taking his turn on the microphone.

"Okay, Claremont. I can't hear you! Are you ready for a Rhino victory?"

I gripped my drumsticks, trying to keep the irritation from creeping onto my face. Couldn't everyone see through this guy? Then he turned to us, extending his hand. "Well give it up for your very own band, led by Miranda Walker. The WallyWackers."

Yeah, he said *Wackers*. But there was no time to worry about him, not with the whole school watching. We banged into a bass heavy version of our fight song, Miranda taking liberties with the lyrics none of us knew, but I would guess did not include the phrase, *Pass, run, score a homerun.*

It didn't matter, the crowd ate it up. And I had to give it up to Claremont. They were full of team spirit. Back in Plattsburgh, our version of a pep rally was a bonfire down the hill behind Reston Field House with the rest of the team, a few shivering parents sipping coffee and looking miserable.

And maybe the funniest thing of all was that *we* were huge, maybe even bigger than the team itself. Afterwards, kids bypassed the meatheads to track us down like we really were on tour. Miranda got most of the attention, but a few high fives came my way too. Taking down my set, I grinned as Megan sliced through the crowd and over to Jaylen with a shiny smile on her face, throwing an arm around him and gushing. Jaylen's smile lit up the gym. Brice had his little fan club, but he didn't look so pleased about it. I just laughed. Sports are great and all, but nothing beats being in a band.

Yeah, I guess we were a band.

CHAPTER 26

I punched the button on my phone, sending a text to Miranda when Vicki arrived at our house. Maybe three minutes later Miranda drifted in, out of breath, pretending to be surprised to find company. Again with the acting, Miranda's theatrics were over the top, and I think I caught something of a British accent in her voice. I cringed and tried to steer her toward the door.

"We're going to go outside to work on some song lyrics."

Vicki turned around on the couch, her chin on her wrist. "So I've heard lots of things about this band. I can't wait to see you guys in action."

Miranda smiled, taking a modest kick at the floor before breaking away from me and striding over to the couch. "Well, it's Mr. Dufresne's guitar playing that's the real show," she said.

Dad scoffed. "Yeah, I don't think so."

Vicki placed a hand on Dad's arm. "I always pegged you for a rock star." Dad blushed, smiling like a goof. I tugged on Miranda's hand.

"Hey Dad, we're going outside."

"Okay, but I'm going to start the grill in a few so hang close."

When I finally managed to drag Miranda outside, she gushed, "Oh my gosh, your dad has a girlfriend!"

"Not a girlfriend, just... I don't know."

Miranda smiled, her eyes trailing back to the door. "Whatever, she's totally into him."

Since our big "breakthrough" or whatever, Dad had asked me over and over about it. The *it* being he and Vicki hanging out. Of course I was okay with it. I was more upset about how Miranda had been right all along. All she did was gloat about it.

The weather was in the high sixties and the colorful leaves were starting to cover the grass. I looked warily up to Mr. Jacobsen's Oak trees. It wouldn't be long before he'd want me over there catching leaves before they hit the ground.

"So, have you asked anyone to the dance?" Miranda said, pulling her knees up on the chair.

I shrugged to look cool. It wasn't cool. "Uh, no. I don't really dance."

"Oh right, Mr. Cool. Well," she shrugged, "I'm sure you have some options after the pep rally."

I started bumbling about something when Dad peeked out onto the porch. "Hey Miranda, did you want to stay for dinner? I've got steaks."

Miranda beamed. "I'd love to. I just need to text my mom."

"Right, I'll put it on," Dad said. I had to admit, it was fun to watch him so giddy and upbeat. When he ducked back inside Miranda grabbed my hand.

"He's excited!"

"Oh boy."

Miranda dropped my hand to take a swipe at my arm. "Stop it, this will be fun," she said, raising her brow.

We ate dinner out on the back deck, Dad and Vicki discussing work and occasionally looking to us with talk about the band. It was weird and great at the same time. Miranda kept stepping on my foot whenever Vicki laughed at one of my dad's corny jokes.

"So you guys play James Brown and soul music. Impressive."

"Well, and some other stuff," I added.

"Yeah, we're working on an original," Miranda said, and my leg flexed.

"Really?"

Dad placed the steaks on the table, diamond cut to perfection along with two large vegetable packs. He looked at Vicki. "Can I get you anything else, my lady?"

My head fell to my palm, but only for a second because my foot was crushed. I grunted and Miranda looked at me sideways. Vicki said she was fine, and for a moment they just sat there staring at each other like goofballs.

"Well, this is nice," said Vicki looking around. "Like a double date."

I coughed, blushed, then shook my head, refusing to look at Miranda. "Oh, uh, we're not dating."

Miranda gasped, cranking up the soap opera-quality drama again. "What? You said I was your girlfriend!" Dad came to my rescue, slapping a vegetable packet on my plate.

"Yeah, you guys are bandmates."

Vicki's eyes went wide. "That's right, The Wallywalkers. I love it." She smiled at Miranda.

"My dog's name is Wally, he's like the band mascot, I guess. Trevor came up with it."

From there, Miranda continued to stomp at my foot until I wasn't sure I could walk on it. She and Vicki talked about all sorts of girl stuff while I managed to polish off my entire steak. It wasn't long though, before the conversation made it back around to the band and then, the fund raiser. Vicki must have thought we really were rock stars or something.

"And you guys are playing the Fall Bash? That's so cool!"

Dad wiped his mouth with his napkin. "Two weeks, I registered our band a couple of days ago. There are already eleven bands playing in this thing."

"Wow. Is there anything I can do to help?" Vicki asked.

"Sure, you can come out and support us," Miranda offered.

"And Jaylen said we could use someone to help out with donations," I said.

Dad coughed and wiped his mouth again. "All right, let's not start recruiting," he said, but Vicki shook her head.

"No, it sounds fun. I'm in."

After dinner, I walked Miranda down the street. The night was cool and the moon bright behind the passing clouds. We started down her driveway when she turned to me. "Well, I was thinking, if you don't want to do your dad's song, that's fine. I don't want to force you guys if you're uncomfortable."

"I don't know. Now that it's out in the open, it's easier. I'll talk to him about it."

Even in the dark I could see her big smile brighten with mischief. "So what do you think about Vicki?" she asked and I smiled back. When Miranda smiled, you smiled. It was impossible to fight it.

"I don't know, she's nice, I guess."

"Yeah, she is nice. And she really likes your dad."

"How do you know?"

Miranda nudged my arm with hers. "Girls know these things."

Wally started barking like crazy as we approached the porch. When we got there, Miranda turned to me, surprising me with a hug. I hugged her back, breathing in the berry-smell of her hair before she broke away.

"Goodnight."

THE NEXT MORNING, Dad and I drove the Blue Ridge Parkway and even climbed Sharp Top Mountain, a forty-minute hike to the highest peak in Virginia. Sitting on the rocks, the view was incredible. It was clear, and we could see for miles, the cars and houses were like tiny dots and patches of squares. Dad wiped the sweat from his forehead.

"Wow, nice up here, huh, Jack?"

I nodded. It was quiet, and the breeze swirled through the brisk air. I was kind of glad it was just him and me, he had mentioned something about Vicki tagging along, and as nice as she was, Dad and I needed the time together. Besides, I still had to ask him a question.

"Hey Dad, can I ask you something?"

"Yeah," he said, looking across the valley, his hand shielding his eyes from the sun.

"Well, there's a song you wrote, in your journals. A poem, I guess, the one about Mom?"

He turned to me, squinting. The wind whipped like crazy, but being up there it felt like we owned the world. "It's really good, Dad. I was thinking we could play it. You know, if you're okay with it?"

His glance returned to the view and he didn't say anything for a while. Then he set his hand on my shoulder, breathing in the fresh mountain air. "I don't know if I'm ready for that, Jack."

I nodded. "It's that song you play though, isn't it? The words go perfectly with it."

"Yeah, but, I never planned on really...*playing* it..." His voice trailed off. I took a breath and kept going.

"It might help, to get it out. But if you don't want to..."

"It might, huh?" he smiled.

A plane roamed overhead, shifting our attention. And sitting up there with him, the blue skies sprawling over the ridges in the distance, it felt like I'd conquered this state. Or at least conquered whatever had come between us since we'd gotten here.

Actually, it felt like we'd conquered the world.

CHAPTER 27

All those good feelings came crashing down on Monday morning when it took everything I had not to pummel Brice Wilkins. I was talking with Miranda in the hallway before homeroom, she was explaining how Trevor's latest science experiment had exploded and nearly set the house on fire—something to do with hydrogen, a balloon, and a welder's torch—when Brice eased right up beside her, reeking of arrogance and cockiness. "Hey Miranda."

Miranda turned and scooted back a step. "Oh, hey Brice."

He nodded to me. "What's up, drummer boy?"

I flashed a grin. "Hey, tough loss out there last week."

His eyes flashed. I'd been paying closer attention to the football team, you know, for moments like these.

Miranda shot me a *I-can't-believe-you-just-said-that* look as Brice turned to her. "So Miranda, I was wondering if you wanted to go to the dance with me?"

My heart hiccupped. *Seriously?* Stunned, I tried to stay cool. But what if she said yes? I'd be left hanging there like a jackhole.

Two seconds, as kids passed and lockers shut. I could hardly breathe. Three seconds, with both Brice and me staring intently at Miranda. Five seconds, as the bell rang. Seven seconds, and Miranda looped her arm around mine and tilted her head at Brice in mock disappointment. "Oh, well I would, but I've already told Jack I was going with him. Right Jack?"

My sudden big cheese grin bounded off the polished floors,

ricocheting off the walls and bouncing down the breezeway. "Uh, yep, that's right," I said proudly. "The dance. We're going."

Brice's cocky grin fell like an anvil. I'm not sure Mr. Popular was used to dealing with rejection, because most of the girls around here would've jumped at the chance. But Miranda was not most girls.

He recovered admirably, shrugging it off with a snort. "Oh, cool. Well, I'll see you guys there."

He turned around and made a quick retreat, peeking back at us a few times as he slunk off. Miranda smiled at me. "It's probably good for his ego to take a hit or two, don't you think?"

"Or three. Or four..." Miranda unlocked her arm from mine and slapped my shoulder. But I was still cheesing. "Hey, it looks like you just blew your chances with the quarterback."

Miranda rolled her eyes, fixing her backpack. "Did I tell you that jerk called Trevor a nerd? I mean, yes, Trevor *is* a nerd. But he's *my* nerd, you know?"

"He's the coolest nerd I know."

WHEN I GOT HOME, Dad was waiting for me, smiling and rubbing his hands together, talking about a surprise. Before I could ditch my book bag, he'd already snatched up his car keys. He let me grab a quick snack then shoved me out the door and led me to the car, refusing to tell me where we were headed. Something about a taste of home.

We weaved through town before turning into a side entrance at Flynn College, where we circled the entire campus twice and got lost until we found a parking spot outside an enormous building called the Powell Center.

Dad leaped out, and I followed him to the trunk. He was still smiling like a goof, like he did when he quoted old comedies he'd watched a hundred times. When he popped the trunk, I saw my skates, my Rangers' jersey, and the rest of my hockey gear. He snatched up one bag and motioned to mine. I was smiling before I could get the question out. "We're skating?"

"Come on, let's go."

The clack and slash of the blades on the ice was like an old friend I hadn't seen in ages. The rink was brand new, enclosed with sleek glass and a huge scoreboard overhead. The lights even worked. Dad smiled as the Jeff guy who'd been over at our house a few times came rushing over and playfully bull-rushed him. His beard had doubled in size since the party, crawling into his nostrils. When he turned to me, his massive hand swallowed my own. While you could tell Jeff was a nice guy, he was also not the dude you wanted to drop your gloves with on the ice.

Turned out, Jeff was an assistant coach with the girls' hockey team, which meant he had full access to the facilities. He showed us to the bench just as a rush of bodies hit the Plexiglas with a bang. Home sweet home.

"Man, I'm glad you guys came," he said in his gravelly voice. He pointed out to the ice where a team was finishing up practice, huddled together as the coach spoke.

"Club team. They're almost done," Jeff said. "Go ahead and lace up." He glanced at his watch then smiled at Dad. "We've got an hour until the girls take the ice, so have at it, old man."

Man, it felt good to be gliding on the ice again. The scoreboard flashed GOAL! and the organ music cranked overhead. Dad looked over at me and laughed. "Just like back home, huh?"

Sort of, I guess. After a while, Jeff joined us with sticks, tossing a puck to the ice and throwing a light forearm my way. "Let's see what you got, blondie."

For the next hour we took penalty shots, and I forgot all about the band, Brice, school, and the dance with Miranda. We laughed and joked and everything faded away. Dad was rusty, and I beat him 5-4 on penalty shots, which I'd only managed to do twice in my whole life.

"You know I used to let you win. Now I can't buy a victory."

Jeff chugged over to talk to someone with the team. Dad and I glided toward the net and he glanced over to me. "You should have seen your mother out on the ice, she was like an angel."

"Really?"

Dad burst out laughing. "No, she was a complete wreck out there, couldn't stay upright. I took her skating for her birthday one year, it was a disaster. She fell face first on the ice, split her lip." He touched his chin.

"Seriously? On her birthday? Good job, Dad."

"Yeah, not my greatest moment, but she forgave me. She was too sweet to hold a grudge. Felt awful though, and I couldn't kiss her for a few days afterwards, so I guess it was my punishment. Never got her back on the ice after it, though."

The team was showing up for practice. I took one last swipe at the puck. Jeff said we were welcome back any time; he'd even scored us tickets to the game. He and Dad talked work for a minute while I just soaked in the ice from the bleachers.

"That was awesome," I said as we walked out to our car. It was dark, the lights to the football stadium lit up the sky, and I could hear the whistles and then the clack of the helmets. Dad looked over and smiled.

"I thought you'd like that."

At the car, Dad popped the trunk and we dropped in our skates and gear. "Oh Dad, so it looks like I'm going to the dance after all."

He shut the trunk and tossed his keys in the air before snatching them dramatically. "Don't you mean the *stupid* dance?"

"Well, Miranda wants me to go."

"Who else?" he said, climbing into the car.

We stopped at Bruce's Burgers for dinner. I filled Dad in about Brice at the pep rally and his latest stunt, asking Miranda to the dance, while Dad nodded along, letting me rant. But then he shrugged and said maybe Brice was worried the new guy was stealing his thunder.

"You think he's worried about *me?*" I said, a french fry touching my lip.

"Well, yeah. Here you come down and start up a band. Now Miranda's going to the dance with you. I mean, from what you're saying the kid's used to having people fall at his feet, and it sounds like you're seriously messing up his image."

Dad tore into his burger. He had this way of talking to me like a buddy or a kid but sneaking in little parenting lessons. Sometimes it didn't make sense until weeks down the road when I wasn't even thinking about it and then *Bam!* I'd look up and realize what he'd been saying all along.

But he was way off on this one. I took a long, noisy slurp of my drink. "Okay, so what if he *is* worried about me or whatever. It's not my fault," I said, irritation creeping into my tone because it reminded me of what Miranda said about me getting in fights. It was like they were teaming up on me and she wasn't even there.

Dad sat back calmly. "No, it's not your fault, Jack. But it never hurts to try and place yourself in someone else's shoes, that's all."

"He's got really small feet for his size. I mean, like freakishly small."

"Not what I meant."

We ate in silence for a while, watching the crush of lights gathering on the main drag. Dad tapped the table to get my attention. "Oh yeah, so I've been thinking about the song, the one about Ellie—your mom."

I jerked my head away from the window. It was still weird hearing him say the word *mom*.

"Really?"

"Yeah, and well, I think we should give it a try."

"Wait. Really?"

"Why not? If it works, we'll have another song. Plus, I think it would be a nice tribute. She'd want us to do it." He rattled the ice in his drink. "But I'm not singing."

"We've got a singer."

"Amen to that."

I called Miranda as soon as we got home and told her the news. She pierced my eardrum with her scream. "Really? That's so awesome, so we can work on it tomorrow night?"

"Yeah, and..." I heard Mrs. Walker in the background calling her in for dinner.

"Hey, I gotta run."

"Oh, really quick, um, when you told Brice you were going to the dance with me, I mean, are we... Were you being serious?"

I sounded like a fifth grader. But the whole thing had been bugging and I just wanted to be sure. Miranda laughed, and for a moment I wanted to chuck the phone across the room and hide under the bed.

"Yes, I was serious, you dork." Then, "Why, do you not want to go?"

"No, I mean, yes. Yes, I do. I just wasn't sure if you did."

"Well, my mom is a chaperone, so I kind of have to go. And I already told her we were going. So if you back out she'll want to know why. Plus, Jaylen and Megan want to double, sooooo you're sort of stuck with me."

I could think of worse ways of spending my time than being stuck with Miranda. In the background, her mom called for her again. "Well, are we going?" she asked, and I sighed dramatically.

"Well, I'd hate to mess up all these plans. I think I can manage."

"I could always go with Brice," she said then ended the call. I rolled over on my back, hands behind my head, just smiling at the ceiling.

CHAPTER 28

I t took most of my Saturday to rake, tarp, and haul Mr. Jacobsen's leaves, so I had plenty of time to toss around everything on my mind. Back home, the short days of cross-country skiing and snowboarding were just around the corner. Here, the colorful leaves indicated a more gradual change in temperatures. The days were warm, and only by nightfall did the temps take a dip. I had to admit, four seasons was nice, but that didn't mean I had to tell Dad about it.

It was on the way back up the hill after trip eighteen or nineteen when my phone buzzed with a text from Jaylen—he wasn't feeling well and wouldn't be at practice. Strange behavior from our most enthusiastic band member. I called him up and tried to talk him out of it, but he wouldn't budge. Pocketing my phone and wiping my brow, I couldn't help thinking something in his voice was off.

When I was finally finished raking, I shuffled down to the Walkers' house. I knocked on the door and Wally went crazy until Mrs. Walker answered with a solemn hello. I was starting to think the flu bug was making its rounds until Trevor busted in with his trumpet.

"Jack! Check it out, I've been working on a solo piece." He let go with a dizzying burst of sound. Wally went running for cover. I nodded.

"Sounds good, Trev. Hey, is Miranda around?"

"Yeah, she's in her room, but—"

Mrs. Walker kindly asked Trevor to quiet down. He turned

away, moping along toward the kitchen. I looked to Mrs. Walker, whose eyes softened. "Jack, Miranda's a little upset."

"*A lot* upset," Trevor said over his shoulder.

"Oh. Why?"

"Well—"

"Mom, it's okay."

Halfway down the stairs, Miranda stood hugging her sides. She wiped her nose. Her eyes were red and flushed like she'd been crying. "Hey Jack. Look, I don't think I can sing tonight," she said, almost in a whisper.

"Yeah, no problem." I shrugged, wishing I'd called first. "Jaylen already cancelled too," I added. Miranda and her mom exchanged looks. Something was up.

"Is everything okay?" I asked, completely lost. Trevor blasted back into the room, his trumpet packed away and ready to travel.

"Are we ready?"

Mr. Walker entered the living room and set a hand on Trevor's shoulder. "Hey kid, let's see if we can get Wally outside, okay?"

"Well, I'm going with Jack."

"Just for a minute. Let's get Wally some air."

Mrs. Walker invited me in as Trevor fixed his hat and followed his dad out the back. When the door shut, the only sound was the fake laughter of a sitcom on television. Mrs. Walker clicked a button and the screen went blank. I stood there, confused in the silence, waiting for somebody to tell me what was going on. Miranda unclasped her arms and came down the steps.

"So, Megan's mom doesn't feel comfortable letting Megan go to the dance with Jaylen," she said, head down, studying her feet. I glanced at Mrs. Walker, then back to Miranda.

"So they won't be doubling with us?"

Miranda looked up. Her eyes were glistening with tears. "Um, no."

I shifted from one foot to the other. "Is her mom super strict, like one of those no-dances-until-high-school kind of things?"

Nobody laughed. Miranda tilted her head, looking at her mom with pleading eyes. Her mom sort of half-smiled and closed her eyes.

Miranda's face burned with an intensity I hadn't seen from her before. She narrowed her eyes at me. "Megan and Jaylen. Jaylen and Megan. Why would Megan's mom *have a problem* with it? Come on, Jack."

They watched as I fumbled over the equation until I winced. I jerked my head at the weight of my own delayed realization. "No way."

"Yes way." Miranda pounced. "Megan's mom said it was nothing against Jaylen personally, but she doesn't want her daughter going to the dance with *'someone like that'*, end quote." Her voice dripped with venom. She shook her head. "I should go over there and tell her how ignorant she is. I mean, it's never been a problem for Megan to hang out with me. Is my skin a more *comfortable* shade for her? I'd love to hear what she has to say," Miranda hissed, slicing each syllable like her tongue was a sword.

Mrs. Walker exhaled loudly. "Miranda, I don't agree with her decision, but we can't tell people how to raise their kids. And we don't need you starting trouble."

Miranda re-crossed her arms. Her eyes in slits. "No? Mom, it's wrong. It's worse than wrong!"

"I agree honey, but it's not our place."

I stood a few steps inside the house, now really, *really* wishing I'd called. I felt bad for Jaylen but for Miranda too, who was practically shaking with anger. But something in her mother's tone made me think it wasn't the first time this sort of conversation had taken place in this house.

"What did Megan say?" I asked, just to say something. Miranda tossed her head back with a sigh.

"She's mortified. She doesn't want to go back to school."

Then, with two bounding strides, Miranda plopped down onto the couch, her anger sputtering into sadness. She took a breath and looked at me. "I'm sorry, Jack. It's just... It hurts, you know, when people say things or assume things, or stare or smile in your face when really, the whole time they're thinking..."

She wiped her eyes again. I sat beside her, unsure of what I could say or do to make her feel better. The kitchen door swung open and Trevor busted in with Wally, Mr. Walker sidling up beside Mrs. Walker.

"Okay, I'm not stupid and I know what's going on," he announced. Mr. Walker looked to Mrs. Walker with a helpless shrug. Wally stuck his nose to my legs and I scratched his head.

"Trevor, not now okay?" Miranda sighed.

"Okay, but I've seen the documentaries. If the two of you start dating, it spells trouble for the band. We have work to do and no time for lovebirds."

I laughed, embarrassed but relieved Trevor was on the wrong trail. In a way I think we all welcomed his innocence. Miranda covered her smile, and her eyes flashed their normal brilliance through the wet glaze. "Oh my gosh, Trevor, really? We're just going to the dance together, *apparently* just the two of us. Where do you get this stuff?"

"Look, one dance leads to another date, and pretty soon the two of you are having lovers' quarrels at practice. Speaking of practice, what are we waiting for? It's after four."

I looked over at Miranda who shrugged. Mrs. Walker nodded. "I think it would be good. Go sing it out, girl."

Trevor blabbed while Miranda ran upstairs to change

clothes. When she returned a few minutes later, she wasn't much better off, but I could see she was trying her best to give it a go.

The three of us entered my house around five. I heard the reverb of Dad's guitar under my feet. He was playing *the* song. His song. Our song. Mom's song. I looked at Miranda and she smiled. I mouthed "You okay?" and she nodded.

It was tough to play James Brown songs without a bass player, but we tried. And the more we tried the more I thought about how I'd never once had to face a problem like Miranda and Jaylen were facing now. All I knew for sure was that after seeing firsthand the effect it had on Miranda, I wanted to do everything I could to help. It was a big problem, one that couldn't be solved overnight. But if there was a solution, I wanted to be a part of it.

Miranda went through the motions, and I think Dad could tell something was off. My timing on the drums was scattered and Trevor was all over the place, lost in a beatnik fog with his trumpet.

But we hit our staples and found our groove. The music was like a shot in the arm, everyone was in the right place at the right time, and we began to sound like a real band. Taking a break, Dad slumped into the chair, his guitar still around his neck as he pulled out a sheet of paper.

"Okay, Miranda, I'm sure Jack here has already shown you this, and I hear you guys want to do an original." He handed the poem to Miranda. Her eyes grew large.

"Uh, Mr. Dufresne, I think you should sing it, since it's, you know," Miranda said, and Dad laughed like it was the funniest thing he'd ever heard.

"With a voice like yours, you want me to sing? I don't think so."

"Yeah, you should," Miranda pleaded.

"No way. If we do the song, we're going to do it right." He held the paper up. "Let's hear it." She took the lyrics, which I think she knew by heart already, and we took our places. "Okay, on three."

Dad laid down the groove, speeding it up like Mr. Carter had suggested. Miranda closed her eyes and swayed to the music. Then she started singing.

> *I feel your warmth in the sun*
> *Hear your whisper in the wind*
> *You'd want me to carry on*
> *But I don't know where to begin*

Miranda's voice was soft and beautiful, hoarse with the wounds of the day's events. The song grabbed us like it was trying to heal everyone's pain, and when it was over Dad looked at Miranda with astonishment. "That was beautiful, Miranda."

"Thanks, Mr. Dufresne," Miranda said, dabbing her eyes with a finger.

"Are you okay?" Dad asked.

"Yeah, it's just...it's nothing."

Miranda and I locked eyes and Dad let it go, unlike Trevor, who crashed into a cymbal and broke the silence.

"Yeah, they're dating now," he said, nodding at us and shaking his head.

CHAPTER 29

Any great scheme takes great planning. And so, Miranda and I put our heads together, brainstorming as we walked the trails with Wally late Sunday morning. We hammered out a plan that afternoon, tinkered with it in homeroom the next morning, and tried our best to conceal our big, goofy smiles just before lunch.

We knew Megan would go for it. Jaylen, on the other hand, would need some convincing. With two mini pizzas on my tray, we took our places at the "band table." Megan was silent and solemn as she fell into her seat beside Miranda, her shoulders slumped as she studied her lunch. Jaylen took his usual spot beside me. He hadn't said much in computer science, but the fact they were both sitting at our table gave us hope. Besides, the wattage of Miranda's smile pulled us in.

"Hey guys, Jack and I have a plan for the dance," Miranda said bluntly. As expected, the word dance hit the table with a thud. Jaylen sighed, mumbling how he wasn't going as he picked at his sandwich. We were well prepared for Jaylen's suspicions, and Miranda tossed back her hair and went into her horrible actress routine.

"Yes, you are. Only you're going with *me*."

That got his head off the table. Megan's too. She wheeled around to her best friend, shock and disbelief clouding her face. "Um, *what?*"

Miranda smiled. "Relax. Here's how it will go down," she

said, as though unveiling a bank heist. We all leaned in, huddling closer. "Mom and I will pick up Jaylen." Miranda shifted to Jaylen, who looked to me for answers. "Jaylen, I'll be your date, and we'll even take some pictures for scrapbooking." Then she set an arm around my neck, her free hand presenting me like a game show hostess. "Megan, you'll be picked up by a charming, blond haired, blue-eyed boy who is new to Claremont Middle School and happens to be the hot current topic of all the eighth-grade girls."

"Really?" I asked, smiling.

Miranda slapped my arm. "Stay with me here."

Megan cut a look at Jaylen, her confusion morphing into interest. Miranda moved to close the deal. "Okay, then we'll meet up at the gym, exchange dates, and everyone lives happily ever after."

Freddie swooped in, crashing down beside Jaylen. "Hey. What are ya'll plotting?"

Everyone popped up in unison. "Nothing, just talking," Jaylen said, twisting at a braid. He was about as convincing as a wolf claiming to be vegan.

"Yeah right. You guys look like you're planning an escape," Freddie scoffed, patting Jaylen on the shoulder. "Look, just make sure you get me out of here too." He stood up and waltzed over to the lunch line. We resumed our huddle.

Jaylen spoke first. "I don't know, why do we have to sneak around?"

"Because my mom is an idiot." Megan went back to studying her lunch.

Miranda frowned. "She's not, Megan, she just has her own beliefs or whatever." I caught Miranda's eyes. She'd come a long way since Saturday.

"But doesn't it hurt your feelings, too?" Jaylen asked Miranda. Megan and I glanced at each other. Again, before the other day I'd never even thought about this sort of stuff, but it was clear Jaylen and Miranda had not only thought about it but had lived it. Many times.

The three of us turned to Miranda, who took a visible breath. "Yes, Jaylen, it does hurt, to be honest. I mean, I don't know, I've known Mrs. Worley since I was like, seven. She's always been nice to me." She glanced at Megan. "I guess she just has some hang ups. But Megan thinks for herself, and that's what matters."

"She's not some kind of..." Megan trailed off before she could say the words. "She's just... I don't know." She looked down, almost whispering. "I understand if you don't want to go with me now."

Jaylen's face tightened. He set his water on the table. "I didn't say that." He turned to Miranda, his trademark smile intact. "So how is this going to work? I need specifics."

WE HAD a full band on Wednesday. Everyone was there, but our focus was not. Megan joined us, and between songs we huddled to discuss the details of our brilliant plan for the dance. We glided through our set list—even our original—and by six-thirty, just as Mr. Carter left with Jaylen—Megan, Miranda, and I were out on the porch, all of us about to head down to the Walkers' place where Mrs. Worley was supposed to pick up Megan.

Trevor was on the swing and Miranda and Megan were doing these goofy dances like the shopping cart and the sprinkler. Miranda had on Trevor's fedora, bobbing along like a dork when Mrs. Worley's minivan slowed to a halt at the curb. We all stopped and looked at each other.

Miranda tensed. "I thought she was coming at seven?"

Megan shrugged. "Me too."

Miranda tossed the hat back to Trevor. Megan dashed to the van to cut off her mom, but Mrs. Worley started up the sidewalk.

"Mom, hey, are you ready to go?" Megan asked, meeting her in the yard. We were all kind of panicking, because if Mrs. Worley met my dad, she might start asking questions about the dance. And if she started asking questions about the dance, our plans were sunk.

"Well, I wanted to hear the band, but it looks like I'm too late. Is this where Jack lives?" she asked, eyeing the house. Her eyes found me. She looked normal, I mean, I didn't know what to expect, but she wasn't exactly the monster I'd made her out to be in my head. She had curly brown hair and wore typical mom-fashion clothes. I took a few hesitant steps down the stairs, brushing the hair from my face.

"Hi, Mrs. Worley, I'm Jackson, or Jack."

"Heya Jack." We shook hands and then her eyes trailed up the steps and over the house. So, is your mom or dad home?"

"Yeah, I'll go get my dad."

I rushed up the steps, flustered and needing Miranda to take control of things. Inside, I found Dad in the kitchen, flipping through his phone and talking to himself. "Dad, uh, Megan's Mom wants to meet you."

"Uh, okay," he said, setting the phone down.

I had to choose my words carefully, but there was no time to think. "Oh, and there's been a change of plans about the dance. I'm going with Megan."

He stopped short. Now I had his full attention. "Megan? I thought—"

"Dad, I'll explain, just please."

He shot me a look. Crumpled forehead, eyes narrowing. *That* look. "I don't get it."

"Dad, please?"

He didn't budge, only waited for an explanation. I peeked out the door. Miranda was doing way too much nodding and smiling. Dad crossed his arms. "Dad please *what?*"

I turned to face him, my voice low and urgent. "I'm still going with Miranda, but we're picking up Megan. I promise I'll explain. And I'll clean my room."

He made a show of looking around. "Even the cereal bowls?"

"Dad. Yes. Please!"

"Okay," he said rubbing his hands together, "I'm in."

We stepped outside. Mrs. Worley looked up and smiled. Miranda and Megan bore holes into me with their stares.

"Hello." Dad greeted her in his parent voice. Mrs. Worley reached out a hand, her bracelet jingling as Dad took it.

"Hi, I'm Crystal, Megan's mom. I just thought I'd stop and say hi, with our kids going to the dance together and all. Looks like I missed rehearsal."

"Wait, I thought you were going with Jack?" Trevor blurted out and Miranda grabbed his arm so hard I thought she'd yank it out of socket. Dad looked at me and then to the pleading faces of Megan and Miranda. "You're so clueless, Trevor," Miranda said out of the side of her mouth.

Dad smiled at Mrs. Worley. "Uh, yes, Jack here's looking forward to it. As a matter of fact, that's all they've been talking about tonight."

"Oh good, because I was worried I had... Well, I just can't believe how fast they grow up." She motioned to the two girls. "I mean, seems like yesterday these two were running around the playground together."

Dad nodded. I glanced over at Miranda, thinking about the hurt and pain in her voice a few days ago. For her to just smile and nod and bear it must have been torture. Dad shuffled on his feet, I can't imagine how confused he was, but he was covering nicely.

"Well, I'll see you on Saturday. Megan tells me that you guys will pick her up. I can help out with anything you need. Right, Megs?"

"Yeah, Mom, can we go now?"

Mrs. Worley shook her head with a laugh. "Always in a rush, this one. Well, it was nice meeting you both. I'll see you on Saturday. Miranda, good to see you, sweetie. Bye."

"Bye, Mrs. Worley."

They climbed into the van and eased down to the bottom of the street. We stood quietly until they sped past and the lights trailed up the road in the gathering darkness.

Dad dropped the act and turned to me. "You want to tell me what that was all about?"

"Yeah, what was that all about?" Trevor said, rubbing his arm.

Miranda patted his head. "Trevor, go home, I'll be there in a minute."

"No way."

"Trevor, please. I need to talk to Jack and Mr. Dufresne. Alone."

Trevor adjusted his hat, swinging his trumpet case. "See? Drama. This is why you don't get involved with bandmates." He shook his head as he shuffled down the walkway, throwing up his free arm. "It never ends well."

Miranda and I each waited for the other to start talking. Dad leaned toward me impatiently. "Well?"

I took a breath and spilled it. Dad's eyes went big as Miranda and I tag-teamed our way through the details. When we finished, the three of us stared at each other. Dad let out a sigh. "That is, uh, that's not at all what I was expecting," he said, puzzled and pacing.

"But will you do it?" I asked. I knew most parents would not have gone with our plan, but my dad did things differently, so I thought there was a chance. There was. He nodded.

"Of course I'll do it." His smile returned. "You guys are impressive, by the way. You came up with this little scheme on your own?" He motioned between us.

We smiled at each other. But Miranda's smile wasn't as big as mine. I realized this wasn't fun and games for her. It still hurt. It always would.

Dad went serious again. "So, just when were you going to tell me?"

"Soon," Miranda said. "I've told my mom, sort of. I mean, I told her I was going with Jaylen. Then she looked at me like I was crazy. But, as a chaperone, she didn't want to know too much so she could plead ignorance."

"I know someone else who could claim ignorance," I said, and Miranda shook her head and smiled at me. Dad got serious on me.

"Okay, so do you want to walk Miranda home before supper, you've got homework to do so hurry."

At Miranda's driveway we both stopped under the streetlight, feeling a rush from our dance with disaster. Miranda grabbed my hand and smiled. "So, it looks like our little plan might work, huh?"

"I think it just might, if—"

Whatever I was going to say was lost. Because she kissed me. She kissed me as we stood under the streetlight in the chilly evening air. One minute we were giggling at our own brilliance, the next her lips were against mine, soft and warm and gone in an instant. My body flushed hot then cold as she pulled away, smiled, and bounced down the driveway, her feet crunching on the gravel as she disappeared into the night.

I stood paralyzed, still tasting the strawberry on my lips, when I heard her voice in the darkness. "Bye Jack."

"Um, goodbye."

CHAPTER 30

As far as couples went, Amanda Miller and Brice Wilkes made sense. She was popular, blonde—even a cheerleader. So when Brice asked Amanda to the dance, they became Claremont royalty.

Maybe it was why Brice was back on his high horse when he and his buddies huddled around me at my locker. It was a shame, too. I'd been in such a great mood after finding one of those little pink notes Miranda sometimes left for me.

"Yo, Jack. What's up, man?"

My jaw tightened. My back shot stiff and straight. I was already running late, and honestly there was no good time for a chat with Brice. He wore his finest showboat smile, nodding his head like his brain played its own theme music. The Brice Show. "So, you excited about the big dance this weekend? Miranda and all?" He looked off to his buddies for laughs.

"I am, and you with uh, what's her name again?" I snapped my fingers. We'd taken to this little routine of trading insults with smiles.

"Amanda," he supplied.

"Oh, that's right, Amanda."

Old Brice seemed especially brash today, like he was itching for a confrontation. And the longer he stood there, the itchier I became too. "Yeah, Amanda. So, are you and Miranda a hot couple now?"

I shuffled the book in my hands, tired of the whole production. "Does it matter?"

He shrugged, pretending to be, in fact, serious. "Hey, maybe you'll even get to kiss her," he said when I'd turned back to my locker. "She's hot man. Even with that, like, birthmark on her cheek."

I slammed my locker and took a step toward him. He flinched, just a little, but enough for me to see. "Funny, it didn't seem to keep you from asking her to the dance, did it?"

Brice glanced at his buddies, whose smirks vanished as they stood wide-eyed and ready to bolt. "Yeah, okay, whatever. That was a joke."

"Oh, it was funny," I said, catching the anger flash in his eyes. He looked back to me, and I thought he'd have the sense to back off. I took a deep breath and grabbed my bag. But he just couldn't let it go.

"Dude, all I'm saying is just aim for the good cheek." He placed a hand on my shoulder that seemed to burn into my bones. I spun around, swiping his hand away.

"Don't touch me," I snapped, about to body check the quarterback when Mr. Sanchez calmly stepped between us. He looked us over, his hands behind his back. Brice threw his arms in the air, Mr. Innocent, looking at me like I was deranged.

"Gentlemen, let's run along," Mr. Sanchez said to the jocks.

Brice eased away, eyes wide, still playing up the innocent role as he started down the hall, catching up with Ryan and Danny who'd already slunk off. Mr. Sanchez gave me a nod. "Right this way, Mr. Dufresne."

Great, now I was on my way to the principal's office.

AFTER SCHOOL, Dad and I got our first haircuts since the move. On the way I told him what had happened with Brice. Even my trip to the principal's office. Really, it wasn't all that bad. Mr.

Sanchez explained how it was his first year at the school too, and he was actually sort of cool. He let me off with a warning, but it felt more like he just wanted to chat about the band.

Dad and I talked about Mom, how he thought our plan reminded him of something she would pull. We'd begun referring to the journals like a novel. *Did you read the part about this?* Or, *wait until you read that.*

But as I watched blond curls fall to the floor, the nerves took hold. The dance attire was announced as "casual," which left a ton of questions. But then there was Miranda, the kiss, Brice and his crew. My trip to the principal's office. Not to mention the plan.

Shoot! The plan!

I sent Miranda a text to make sure everything was still on.

She sent one back. Everything was a go.

CHAPTER 31

Megan answered the door wearing a fluffy dress secured with a belt. She gave Dad and me a mischievous smile, and for a second I thought we could just get going. Didn't happen. Mrs. Worley invited us in, wasting no time with the camera. Megan and I posed, stiff as mannequins in front of the fireplace while her mom snapped away. "Sorry, I take pictures of everything."

Megan stamped her feet. "Mom, no Facebooking!"

"Aw, just one, Megs?"

"Mom! No."

Things were awkward enough already. I'm not sure Megan and I had ever said a word to each other without Miranda or Jaylen around, but Mrs. Worley was a maniac, zipping about with her phone, going on about how cute of a couple we were. Even Dad started checking his imaginary watch and inching for the door.

Eventually, Megan wrangled away from her mom and we made our way to the car with a few minutes to spare. We took a collective breath of relief. Phase one was complete.

"Well, we made it," I said to Megan as we pulled out onto the street.

"I feel like an accomplice to a crime," Dad said, eyeing the rearview.

"Well, you are the getaway driver!" Megan laughed. Dad grimaced as we drove off, Megan's mother waving to us from the door.

The school parking lot was nearly full as we pulled up to the curb where Miranda waved us over. Jaylen stood at her side, looking sharp in a button-down shirt. Megan couldn't help her giggles. Now that her mother had forbidden her to go with him, combined with the fact he was in a band, Jaylen had been elevated to rock star status. As Dad slowed the car, Megan turned to me, her hand on the door latch. "Well, Jack, looks like this is where we part."

I started to say something as we got out of the car, but Miranda sauntered over to us, and I took in her knee length skirt, jean jacket, the flower tucked into her hair just behind her ear. Everything I'd worried about evaporated. As did my vocabulary.

"Um, wow. You look amazing."

"And you clean up nicely." Miranda laughed, nodding to my hair, or, where my hair used to be.

I ran a hand over my head. "It's short."

"I think it looks handsome."

My whole face went hot. "Really?"

"I like it," she said, and suddenly I did too. Miranda nodded to Jaylen and Megan. "So it looks like we've both been dumped," she said, and we laughed, glancing at the happy couple whispering to each other and giggling.

"Yep, so far so good."

Dad, having done the unspeakable act of exiting the vehicle, waved to Mrs. Walker, who was manning the door. Then, to my horror, he came over and clapped my back. "Jack, have fun, I'll be back at eight. Right here at eight, okay?"

"Yeah Dad, sure," I said through gritted teeth. He turned back for the car, and I thought about what he'd done for us. "Oh, and thanks for everything."

Dad shrugged. "Anytime."

Mrs. Walker waved us in. Miranda called over to Jaylen and Megan. "Well, let's get inside."

Inside, the lights pulsed with the music, dappling the bleachers with purple and pink dots as a laser show bounced off the floor. We were maybe two steps in when Miranda was caught by the current of screaming girls rushing out to the dance floor. She looked back at me with a smile. All I could do was wave.

I went looking for Megan and Jaylen, stopping off for chips and a soda, when I ran into my favorite quarterback.

"Look at that hack job!"

Brice. It never ended with this guy. I pretended not to hear him over the music, sipping my soda. Not that it stopped him. "Man, they really scalped you." He glanced at Amanda with a smile, then made a show of looking around. "Hey, did you lose your date?"

"What?" I gasped, slamming down my soda. "Oh no. Should I post flyers?"

Amanda actually snorted, and Brice's face twisted into scowl, his skin pink enough to match his button-down shirt. I sucked down the rest of my drink, eyeing the exit, when Miranda returned from the group-dance.

She slipped in, flushed from all the dancing. "Okay, I'm not quite ready for all of that yet!"

Brice composed himself and nudged Amanda toward the rest of the football players. When he was gone, she looked at me. "Is everything okay?"

"Yeah, it's just—"

"What? Brice? Don't waste your time. Come on." She grabbed my arm, and I tried to forget about what he'd said about kissing her. I didn't want to let him ruin my night. Thinking about all of that, I didn't realize Miranda was leading me out to dance until it was too late.

We found Megan and Jaylen on the dance floor. I sort of bobbed around as the four of us broke into four separate dances. I laughed as Jaylen came up with a wild, flailing motion that looked like his back was on fire. Then we started up with our porch dances. I did the sprinkler and Miranda joined in with the shopping cart and soon others fell in line with the golf swing, the lawn mower, and everything else.

A couple times I spotted Brice watching from the shadows, arms crossed and face red. Amanda looked bored.

Then the music slowed. The dance floor began to clear out. Only the brave remained. Miranda looked at me and shrugged. *Okay*, I thought. *Here goes.* I took a breath, stepped forward, and carefully placed my hand on Miranda's lower back.

We swayed to the music, occasionally peeking over at Jaylen and Megan. "I think we did the right thing," she said.

"Yeah, I think so."

She lifted her face from my shoulder, gazing into my eyes. I smiled, but Mrs. Walker stood a mere thirty feet away, staring like a sniper.

"Jack."

"Yeah?"

"You're drumming on my back."

"Oh, sorry."

I tried to think of something to do with my hands as I breathed in the sweet smell of Miranda's hair. Another slow song—two in a row. But it wasn't so bad, Miranda laughed and made jokes. We talked about Jaylen and Megan, swaying under the glittering lights. It was nice. The plan, the band, and the girl. Everything was working out. At least until Miranda froze with nothing but pure terror in her eyes.

I followed her gaze. "Um, is that?"

"Oh no."

Mrs. Worley stood like a mannequin beside Mrs. Walker.

The music faded and DJ Bob (seriously) announced the poster design contest finalists. Miranda's gaze dropped in resignation, and slowly we followed Megan and Jaylen toward Mrs. Worley.

"Mom, what are you doing here?" Megan yelled over the noise. Her eyes were glossy, and I thought things might get ugly as a few heads turned our way. But Mrs. Worley was calm.

"Can I talk to you both. In private?"

If I were in Jaylen's shoes I would have been eyeing an escape route, looking to flee the scene by way of fire exits or air vents. But he simply looked her in the eye and said, "Yes, ma'am."

As the poster contest began, the fast music returned, blaring and happy—which was the exact opposite of what I felt watching the three of them walk through the double doors and into the bright hallway.

"Mom, what's going on?" Miranda's voice shook, and I thought she might start yelling. Mrs. Walker put a hand on her arm.

"It's okay, honey, I think this is a good talk."

I hoped so. The lights swirled around us, tattooing the walls. The poster winners were announced to a blast of cheers and screams. Miranda and I stared at the doors. Brice and the football players tossed around a stuffed teddy bear like a football. Amanda laughed with some friends at the refreshment table. I looked back at Miranda, who gave me a nervous smile.

Two horrendous songs later, Miranda slapped my arm as Megan and Jaylen emerged through the doorway. They returned to the floor as Mrs. Worley took her place in the back near the wall with a throng of other parents. Nobody was crying at least, so that was a good thing.

"Everything okay?" Miranda asked, and Megan looked at Jaylen and smiled.

"Yeah, as good as it can be."

Megan and Miranda huddled in a corner, Megan wiped her eyes and gushed with laughter. I looked at Jaylen, busy with a braid as we walked over to the refreshments.

"So what? Everything's cool now?"

He shrugged. "I don't know about cool, but she apologized. She said something about it was the way she was raised. She said the more she thought about it the more ashamed she felt. Said she didn't want to raise her daughter the same way."

"Wow, so she just decided to come out to the dance and apologize?"

"Yep, she said she knew something was up."

"Maybe our plan wasn't as great as we thought."

"Or maybe you need to work on your acting skills."

He laughed, but I was too surprised about everything to smile. I looked over to Miranda and Megan. Miranda was nodding and smiling. When she saw me looking, her eyes widened as if to say, "Can you believe this?"

Jaylen grabbed my shoulder. "Oh, and she said she knew I was a good kid, and she wanted to tell me face to face."

"Man, you've got her fooled."

He raised an eyebrow with his smile. "Right?"

We grabbed a couple of drinks and the lights dimmed. Then DJ Bob once again took to the microphone. I wasn't really paying attention until I heard "Wallywalkers" and then there were a few cheers in the crowd. I looked at Jaylen, who smiled before, out of nowhere, James Brown's raspy voice filled the gym.

Mind. Blown. My jaw fell open and Jaylen mouthed, "I Feel Good." I spun around and we scanned out to the floor where Megan and Miranda were frantic, waving us over. We exchanged shrugs, gulped down another soda, wiped our mouths, then tossed the cups in the trash.

Jaylen set a hand on my shoulder. "Let's go get our dates."

For the next half hour we danced. Everyone. We had a dance off, and I even broke out the worm. The girls screamed and laughed when we tried to breakdance, and Miranda showed me up big time with her own moves. By the time Mrs. Newton broke us up so nobody would get hurt, the lights had come on but we still had a small crowd watching and cheering. Even Amanda had joined us out there.

Poor Brice.

ON THE WAY HOME, I gave Dad the play by play. Miranda filled in the details as I jabbered through the highlights about how Megan's mom had busted us and ended with James Brown. Dad blinked, trying to keep up. Pulling down to the end of the street, he stopped at Miranda's driveway, under the basketball hoop. I hopped out and told Dad I'd be home in fifteen minutes. He gave me five.

"So, that went, uh, well," I said, realizing this was the first time we'd been alone all night.

"Yeah," Miranda said, leaning on my shoulder for balance as she unstrapped her shoes. She breathed a sigh of relief. "Oh, man. These things are evil," she said with the shoes in hand. It was so quiet out in the dark, and the night was still ringing in my head.

"Hey, are you okay?" Miranda asked.

"Yeah, it's just something Brice said."

"What, how he tried to kiss me at Goonies?"

I took a step back. "Wait. How did you know?"

She rolled her eyes. "I figured he'd try to make you jealous. Well, he kissed me all right, over summer, that night downtown? He said he needed to talk to me. I mean, we were walking along, and then as soon as we were behind the trees he reached over and tried to plant one on me. I clocked him though."

"Wait, you like..." I made a swinging motion.

"Yeah, slapped him good. Why, what did you hear?"

I shook my head, unable to stop laughing. "Nothing. You slapped him? Really?" I said and she gave me a funny look. But it made sense now. Miranda was the one girl who was immune to his charm and *that's* why it drove him crazy. And the fact she'd smacked him down when he tried to put the moves on her just made it all the sweeter. I stepped closer to Miranda without thinking. The streetlight buzzed and she arched her brow with a smile.

She saw me looking at her cheek, the right one with the birthmark, a slight patch of darker skin about the size of my thumb. She turned away. "Don't."

"What?"

"I hate it."

"Miranda, I wasn't looking at it."

"Then how do you know what I meant?"

"I mean, I wasn't looking at it in a bad way." I shrugged. "I like it."

I did. She was so perfect in every way, the mark only added to her charm. It kind of made her real. But I don't think she felt the same because she sighed and gave me a generous roll of the eyes. Her shoulders sagged.

"I want to get it removed. When I'm eighteen."

"I think it makes you, *you*."

"People are really mean though."

"Some. But there's always going to be jerks, right?"

She smiled her perfect white smile that made me flush but keep on blabbing. "When I first saw you, I thought, wow, that girl is really pretty. Not, oh, she has a birth mark."

The smile widened even more as she tapped my shoulder. "You did not."

"Well, maybe the first thought was, 'wow her brother sure talks a lot,' but after that."

I leaned closer. When she looked up her face was serious.

"What?" I asked, and she looked right into my eyes, nodding the hair out of her face.

"I was wrong about you. You're nothing like Brice," she said, and it was my turn to look away. She pointed at my chest. "Jack Dufresne," she said dramatically, in a deep voice. "Your name sounds important."

"Um, like how?"

"I don't know," she giggled. "It sounds like a character in a book or something. Detective Jack Dufresne."

"Putting bullies in their place one day at a time..." I joined in and we both started cracking up, still warm in the cool night. Then a sweep of headlights fell over us.

The sniper.

"It's my mom." Miranda backed away, and the van cruised down to where we stood, flustered and surely looking guilty as ever. Mrs. Walker leaned out the window.

"One last slow dance?"

"Yeah." We said at the same time, our eyes on the street, waiting to be scolded. But Mrs. Walker was still wired from the cleaning.

"Wow, so how about that whole thing with Megan's mom?" she said, and I could only nod because my mind was too foggy at the moment to say anything meaningful. She continued on. "And you should have seen the mess in the gym. I've never seen such trash. Cups, plates, streamers, all sorts of stuff." She went on about cleaning up and the mess and I just stood there, thinking how Miranda's kiss had been lost in the night. After giving us an inventory on how many sodas were consumed, she looked at Miranda.

"Well, sweetie, it's getting late," she said, and then looked down at the ground. "And honey, your poor feet." Miranda bent down, fixing her shoes on her feet. Mrs. Walker turned to me, the glow of green from the dashboard illuminating her cheek. "Oh, Jack, we're going to the corn maze tomorrow if you and your dad want to join us."

I looked at Miranda who shrugged. "Wanna go be lame with us?"

"Sure."

"Okay, well, see you tomorrow, I had fun tonight," she said before hopping in. Mrs. Walker smiled at me before driving off.

"Good night, Jack."

"Good night."

CHAPTER 32

I strolled into the Computer Cave on Monday morning, still soaring from the weekend. First, the dance on Friday, and then getting lost in a corn field with Miranda on a cloudless Saturday afternoon. Dad and I vegged out on movies Sunday. Altogether, not a bad deal.

The Wallywalkers were only a week away from our big debut. I used my two minutes before the second bell to check out the Fall Bash website, to scope out if any new bands had joined, and because I liked seeing *The Wallywalkers* on the lineup.

Jaylen nudged me, leaning close to whisper. "Hey man, there are uh, some rumors going on about you."

"Oh yeah. I've got a record deal and I'm leaving the band?" I laughed. Jaylen shook his head without smiling.

"No. Dude, I'm being serious."

I closed out the website. Mr. Coleman walked in and fired up the smart board. Jaylen waited until he turned his back again. "It varies, but mostly it's about your mom. That she left your dad. Then I heard she was in rehab. But the latest was that she was in a mental institution."

A stab of anger jarred me loose when he said *mom*. I shrugged it off, determined not to let it get to me. Who cared what these dunces thought? The whole school was full of followers, with little pockets of groups and those not quite in the group but just hoping to get in.

But as much as I told myself it didn't matter, I didn't care, I couldn't help but notice the lingering glances, couldn't help hearing the hushed whispers in the hallways. I cinched up my book bag, lowering my shoulders and daring anyone to get in my way as I powered through the crowd.

I marched into gym class just as the bell rang. Mr. Hatch was busy with a custodian, a mop bucket, and a mystery substance near the water fountains. I had an audience. All three gym classes sat on the bleachers because it was a free day and we didn't have to dress out. When I found Brice with Ryan and Danny I headed straight toward him. Everyone got quiet as I approached. Brice leaned back, trying to be cool, but I saw a hitch in his smile.

I gave him a head nod. "Hey Brice, can I talk to you for a minute?"

He looked around and laughed. "About what?"

"It'll just take a second. Come on." I motioned for him to follow me, knowing he would because all eyes were glued to us. He wouldn't want to look like a chicken in front of his buddies, so with a forced grin he followed me to an empty corner of the gym.

"What's up, Jack?" he asked. No *Drummer Boy* or *Wally Wacker*. Just Jack. The bleacher section leaned in unison for a better view. I closed the space between us.

"My mom's dead. She died in a car accident when I was three." I said it as calmly as I could manage. I wanted to keep my voice steady so he knew he hadn't riled me up, but I wasn't doing so hot.

His eyes darted around the gym, then to his feet. "I...uh, okay?"

"I just wanted you to know the truth. There are lots of rumors going around," I said. Behind Brice, in the distance, Miranda stood near the bleachers, watching closely.

"Rumors, pfft. I didn't say anything, man. I don't even know what you're talking about," he spluttered. I nodded my head.

I started to walk away, but something else came to mind. I spun around and he jerked back a step. "Oh yeah, and Miranda told me the truth. About what happened at Goonies, so...."

He bristled like he wanted to say something. But I laughed in his face. Whatever calmness I'd gathered in the courtyard had evaporated. If he wanted to make a move, I was all for it. I heard my grandpa's voice, how he used to say if a kid wants to yap, he'd better be ready to scrap, and with that I stepped forward to him again. "Look man, if there's anything you want to say in the future, you know where to find me." With that, I stomped off, satisfied with my tough guy line.

At the bleachers, Jaylen hustled over from the basketball courts. "Dude, what was that all about?"

"Just getting the facts straight."

But if I thought I'd scared Brice off, I was wrong. By the next day, the rumors had not only continued, but gotten worse. Let's see, I'd been expelled for fighting. I'd been released from a detention home before Claremont. Oh, my mom had left my dad because she was scared of me. And on it went.

After two days of nonstop rumors it was all I could do not to fight the entire school. When Miranda sat down at the lunch table, I asked if she'd heard all the stuff being said about me, but she just nodded, like it wasn't important.

"Jack, you have to let it go." She gestured to Jaylen and Megan. "We know the truth. Who cares what people think?"

I sighed, sick of being told to let it go. I guess when you're pretty and popular like she was it was no problem. "Easy for you to say," I blurted out. "Nobody's calling you a psycho or talking about your dead mother."

Miranda's lips parted. She cocked her head with a bitter laugh. "So you think you're the first person to have stuff spread about you? Is that it, Jack?"

I studied the table, turning over my ham and cheese sandwich. Dad had gone wild with the mustard, and it was all over the bag so there was no way to get it out. Not that I had an appetite, anyway. I'd just stuffed my foot in my mouth.

I took a breath and raised my eyes to hers. "That's not what I meant. I just…"

She held her up a hand, but it was the anger in her eyes that stopped me in my tracks. "Try being adopted, Jack. Try having your parents come to the school play and everybody asking you why you don't look like your mom or your dad or your brother. No, Jack. Gee, I suppose I wouldn't understand this rumor thing at all."

I could've slid into the cracks in the floor with the millions of crumbs from the years of past lunches. Jaylen and Megan looked away. There was nothing else to say. I closed my eyes and whispered, "Miranda, I'm sorry. It's not what I meant."

"What does it matter?" she said, wiping her eyes, turning away.

"Miranda."

She shrugged, eyes brimming. Our table went silent. Brice, over at his table, whooped it up without a care. I looked around, wondering why some people got away with everything, even trashing people for their own amusement before moving on to the next target. I was just the attraction at the moment, next year it would be someone else. But looking at Miranda, I thought about Brice's birthmark comment, and it was easy to see what their little game left behind.

When I got home, I crawled out my bedroom window to the little perch on the roof, thinking about the stupid school and the stupid students and all the stupid things I'd thought were so important. How could anyone say so much as a mean word to Miranda? Then a realization hit hard. It made me drop my head between my knees.

I looked to the sky, remembering what Miranda had first said about Brice and me being alike. How I used to be "the guy" at my old school. I hoped I'd never made anyone feel like I did now. But I couldn't shake the feeling that I had.

Dad's car drifted down the street, the speakers thumping inside the doors. It made me smile watching him sing along, smacking the steering wheel like he was Keith Moon (the maniac drummer for *The Who*). Dad banged away as he parked, then gathered his bag and shut the door, whistling and singing until he looked up and spotted me.

"Jack. Hey buddy."

"Hey Dad," I said, trying to sound normal, but my voice broke. Maybe it was the way he said, "Hey buddy," how it sounded like Grandpa. Or maybe I was just being a lump. Dad stood on the walkway for a second, studying my face before he hit the steps.

"I'll come up."

The door shut, followed by a thump as he dropped his bag, steps shuffled up the stairs, and a few seconds later my dad was climbing out the window, his work badge dangling from his neck, catching on the window sill.

"Careful Dad, I don't want you to fall," I said sarcastically. He huffed and exhaled, pulling up his knees with his arms.

"Ahh, there we go," he said and then turned to me. "So, how was your day?"

I closed my eyes and let out a deep sigh.

"That bad, huh?"

I nodded.

"Brice again?"

I nodded again. "He's been spreading all sorts of rumors about me. Even about Mom and us. He's telling everyone I was in juvie. He's saying I'm some sort of reject. Dad, it's all I can do not to punch him in the face."

Dad turned to me, his blue eyes catching the sunset as he searched my face. "Let's not punch him in the face, Jack. Okay?"

"You sound like Miranda."

"I wish. I can't sing like that girl," he said, and then took a deep breath, growing serious as we both looked out to Mr. J's great oak trees. "Jack, she's right, as easy as it sounds for me to say, and I'm sure it's hard, you just have to ignore it. I mean, you've got Jaylen and Miranda by your side. And Trevor."

"So what, I let this guy continue to walk all over everyone?"

Another sigh, Dad's face tightened in thought. "Well, if you fight him, or hit him in the face as you said, doesn't it sort of make all the rumors true? That you're nothing more than some crazy bad kid from up North?"

I hated when he did that, changed it up so I was pinned down by my own words. I huffed. "I guess."

The sun had dropped behind the trees and the cooler air felt good in my lungs. I pulled down my sleeves while Dad and I sat in silence for a moment, listening to the evening. Wally barked in the distance, and I thought about him out in the backyard, begging to come in because Mrs. Walker was cooking dinner in the kitchen. Then I looked over to Dad.

"Dad, do you remember Arnie Siedman?" I asked, thinking about the chubby kid back home, one reason I felt so bad about the past. Arnie Seidman was the kid we all used to tease at the pool because he wouldn't take his shirt off.

Dad's forehead wrinkled in thought. "Oh yeah, Arnie. Nice kid."

"We were kind of mean to him, you know? Teasing him and stuff."

"I think I remember him coming over a few times."

Sure, I wasn't personally mean to Arnie, but I never stood up for him either. By middle school, Arnie's weight ballooned and he was called all sorts of newer, meaner names as he roamed the hallways. I looked to my feet. "Dad, I did it too. He used to give me hockey cards and stuff. And I still laughed on the bus."

Dad sighed, grasping on to what I was saying. "And now you're on the other side of it, huh?" I nodded. Dad grimaced. "Jack. You've handled this whole move thing exceptionally well. Not just the move, but everything with us too," he said, putting a hand on my shoulder. Then he leaned his head down to catch my attention. "You can't let this guy get to you, okay? You know that's exactly what he wants, right?"

I nodded. "Yeah. But, I mean, I can understand starting a bunch of rumors about me, I guess. I'm the new kid, and we didn't always treat the new kids back home all so great, but Miranda?" I told him about lunch. Dad listened thoughtfully, like he always did, letting me ramble and get all my jumbled-up thoughts out of my head. Then I felt better, sorta.

"Jack, I'm sure she knows you didn't mean it that way. But think about her. All the questions you have about your mom and how hard it is for us. Think what it's like for her."

"I know, Dad, I messed up. I just hope she'll talk to me."

"She will, Jack. Trust me." He patted my shoulder as he turned to stand. "Now, you want some dinner?"

I shrugged.

"Sure you do."

Dad climbed back into the house, leaving me to gaze down the street in the direction of Miranda's house. Through the thinning trees I could make out the yellow glow of her windows, and I wondered how I could fix everything. Miranda always shined, thinking of others before herself. And while I was busy feeling sorry for myself, she'd been busy trying to show me how my friends were right in front of my face.

I'd been too dense to see it.

CHAPTER 33

I'd just come back in when Jaylen called with an update on the rumors. At the rate they were flying, I thought I might soon need my own twitter feed.

"He's calling you a nut case, said you got expelled. Said they kicked you out of the state for trying to kill a teacher."

"You can't be serious."

"That's not all. He's saying you pulled a knife on him in gym class."

"Like a butter knife or a steak knife?"

"Not sure, I'm just relaying the messages."

I fell into my bed, my hands instinctively reaching for my curls that were no longer there. I stared at the wobbling ceiling fan in my room, trying to be more easygoing, like Dad. But this was getting pretty ridiculous.

"That guy's got some imagination; I'll give it to him."

Jaylen cleared his throat. "But, I mean, didn't you get in some fights up there?"

"Not really. I mean, I played hockey, and sometimes, on the ice, things get a little crazy. Sure, we'd mix it up out there, but come on, Jaylen, you're not buying this stuff too, are you?"

"No man, I'm with you. Now if he'd said you pulled a drumstick on him though..."

"Ha ha."

Dad called me down for dinner. I checked my phone again for missed calls or a text, even though the phone had been sitting in front of my face. I'd left Miranda two voicemails, and then a couple of desperate texts asking how she felt and later, if she was still coming to practice tomorrow.

Dinner wasn't Dad's finest, soupy Spinach Fettuccine served in a bowl. He attempted to lighten the mood with a snarling Elvis impression, one of the better ones in his arsenal. He had three go-to impressions: Elvis, Robert DeNiro, and Donald Trump. There were more, but his Jodie Foster, George W. Bush, and Sean Connery impressions were all the exact same voice. Not only that, I couldn't tell you who Jodie Foster or Sean Connery even were, I'd just never had the heart to tell him.

No point in doing homework, I couldn't stay focused. Like I said, I could deal with the entire school thinking I was crazy, but my stomach rolled with the thought of Miranda being upset with me. It wasn't long before I was back on the roof.

I was only up there a few minutes when I saw her. My heart bashed around like a high-hat as Miranda's long strides swept under the streetlamp. She climbed the steps to our porch, and I scurried back inside and to the steps just as she knocked.

"Hey Jack," she said quietly, looking up. Dad stood at the door.

"Hey."

"Can I uh, talk to you?" she asked. I took a few steps down the stairs, looking to Dad and then back to Miranda.

"Yeah, sure. Dad, can we go upstairs?"

Dad made a face but nodded his approval. Miranda followed me up to my room, where I quickly kicked a dirty sock toward the laundry basket. "The cleaning lady's been sick," I said, trying and failing to make her laugh.

Miranda sighed and bowed her head. "So, I just wanted to say I'm sorry for today, I got a little emotional."

"You don't need to apologize, it was me. You were just trying to help. I was feeling sorry for myself."

She lifted her head. "It's just...it's not always easy being different."

I slid a pair of dirty socks under my bed with my foot. "It seems like everyone likes you."

She rolled her eyes but with a small smile. Then she saw my English book and her eyes flashed. She sat down and ran her hand over the book. "Well, well. Look who's studying."

"Yeah, what sort of delinquent psycho does homework?" I said, and then she *did* laugh. I felt my worry drifting out the window, which I'd left open. She rubbed her arms and I rushed over to shut it, then took a seat at the end of the bed, wondering what else was on her mind. I followed her eyes as they spanned the room.

Miranda jumped up, taking a look around. "This is such a guy's room."

I followed her gaze to my Rangers posters and Ludwig drum set stickers. "What did you expect?"

"I don't know, unicorns and fairies." Yep, the old Miranda was back.

"Sorry to disappoint."

"So," she said, already up and reaching to my closet. "I've been thinking, and what you need is a makeover."

Before I had a chance to stop her she started rifling through my clothes, stopping at a pink striped button down. She arched an eyebrow and looked back at me.

"Makeover?" I said, confused. "What, exactly, do you mean?" I pointed to my head. "I already got a haircut."

She spun back around to my closet. "Well, actually, I like your style," she said, plucking out a striped collared from the rack, one I never wore. "But, we need to work on your image."

"My image?"

She set a finger to her chin. "Hmm. How can I put this

delicately? When you're at school, you walk around like a cave man."

"Wait, I'm sorry?"

"A caveman. A knucklehead. A guy headed to the ring for a boxing match. Should I go on?"

"Well..."

"Yeah, like this." She scrunched up her nose and swayed left to right with her arms dangling. It might have been the funniest thing I've ever seen. I pointed at her.

"Okay, I do not do *that*."

"Yes, you do. "

"Did you call me a *knucklehead*?"

She nodded, waving me off. She picked up the shirts she'd taken from my closet, returned the stripes, and put my pink shirt on right over her long sleeves. It looked really good on her too.

"You're not helping things with your attitude."

"So it's my fault?" I asked defensively. Her expression fell and she tilted her head. I lost track of what she was saying.

"Look Jack, when we're together, down in the woods or at practice, you have this kind of, like, I don't know, this energy about you. A look in your eyes, like, 'I'm the happiest person in the world'. You're funny and sweet," she said softly, and I felt the heat rising to my face.

"But at school," she continued, "you become some big bad tough guy. Mr. 'I can't show people I'm a human' face."

I rolled my eyes and she slapped my leg. "Anyway, I've come up with a plan."

"Right. Because our plans work *so* well..."

She ignored me. "I'm proposing a solution, one I'm calling, Operation *Smile*."

"Operation what?"

"Look. If Brice and his people are spreading all of this stuff about you. About you being a nut, or in juvie, or even a psycho—

what better way to dispel all of it than by just smiling. Kill them with kindness and all."

"Miranda, no offense, but this is the corniest thing I've ever heard."

She twirled, ran a fingertip down the rest of my shirts before spinning around with the widest, most dazzling, brilliant, daughter-of-a-dentist smile yet. My lips spread apart.

"Feels good, doesn't it?"

I shook the smile from my face. "Yes, I guess. But... *Really?*"

Having grasped my full attention, she shut the closet door and dropped down beside me, taking my hands in hers. "Okay, let's say you go to school tomorrow and beat up Brice Wilkins."

"I like where this is going," I said, earning an obligatory eye roll.

"Great, then what? Everybody just thinks all of the rumors are true, and you're just some monster. Is that what you want?"

"So do you and my dad plan these talks, or..."

She swung my hands. "Are you with me?"

I bit my bottom lip, cut my eyes to her. She squeezed my hands, and I peeked at her long, smooth legs. I thought about school. The finger pointing and whispering in the hallways, the rumors and stories floating around about the new kid. If I did pummel old Brice I'd get suspended, which would mean no Fall Bash. Finally, I dropped my head, and then looked up with the biggest cheese grin I could muster. "Fine," I said, through a wall of gritted teeth.

She grabbed my face and looked me in the eyes, and I was lost. "I knew you'd see it my way. Now come on, let's practice smiling." She balanced my textbook on her head with her arms out as she walked to the stairs.

I shook my head. Smiling.

CHAPTER 34

Operation Cheese Grin stormed Claremont Middle School without fanfare or warning. I stepped off the bus the next morning grinning ear to ear. I'd spent last night parading across the living room, smiling until my cheeks were sore as Miranda and Dad took turns judging and laughing. So yeah, I felt like an idiot, but like Miranda said, it wasn't like the rumors could get any worse.

Trevor doubled over laughing as I wound my face up like a lunatic, my smile as sarcastic as it was demented. "You look insane," he said jubilantly.

"Well then, it should fit this plan perfectly."

Our first targets were Sarah Witcher and friends. With a deep breath, I unleashed my pearly whites and watched as hands rose to mouths. They giggled and whispered, but instead of rolling my eyes and plowing ahead, I marched over to them, armed with nothing more than a clown smile.

I spread my arms in greeting. "Hi Sarah, Julie. How are you guys? What a gorgeous fall morning, huh? Brisk even, you just couldn't ask for a better day, could you?"

I could have told them my rocket ship had landed and I was going to the moon, because they looked at me like I was an alien life form. "Uh, hi," one of them managed, and we all stood there, my grin tearing at my cheeks. Finally, Sarah bolted, rushing off to class with Julie and the other girl close behind.

"Okay, well, have a wonderful day, all of you," I called out as they broke away, and before she reached the door, Sarah turned around and I waved again, and she stumbled trying to get inside. Trevor loved it, and I think I even saw a hint of a smile on Julie's face.

"That was crunk!" Trevor said, continuing his latest habit of using outdated slang in the wrong context. "Nice touch with the bow. Let's do some more. Look, how about them!" He tugged at my arm. "The guy with the hat's name is Kevin, and that's Ben beside him, with the hoodie."

Why not? I thought. "Kevin, Ben, hey guys?" I launched into my routine all over again. Sure, I was being a cornball, but I had to admit, it was kind of fun.

Walking into school, I found Miranda at the door, clutching her notebook. She had a gleam in her eyes. "Be careful, Detective Jack. You might actually make some friends."

"I don't think so."

Once in the hallways, my face tightened into its normal position. Miranda's elbow found my ribs. She pointed to her mouth. "Um, where's the smile?"

After first period, Miranda and I parted ways, and I kind of slacked off on the smiling, but to my credit I didn't frown. The whispering and pointing continued, but I tuned it out, nodding and grinning, and after a while I wasn't even doing it sarcastically. Besides, Miranda had spies everywhere.

"Hey cheese face!" Jaylen said, giving me a playful push. "Megan said you're supposed to smile all day. I don't know if I can let that slide."

"You too, Jaylen?"

"I think it's working. I haven't heard anything new today."

"Really? I haven't knocked off a liquor store or robbed any old ladies? I *am* slipping."

We stood in the hallway outside of class. People drifted by, laughing as I smiled and waved like a politician. Jaylen scoffed.

"Whatever man, you know you like it. And besides, you're not going to argue with Miranda anyway."

"Probably not."

The bell rang and we entered the cave. Jaylen let his bag slide to the floor. "Hey, speaking of cheesing, you should have seen my dad's face when I told him about our charity. He was speechless."

"You just now told him?"

Jaylen shrugged. "Well, you didn't exactly get right to the point with your dad either."

I nodded. "I guess you're right. So he's on board?"

"I think so. My mom started crying. We checked out the website. Dude, there are like fifteen bands playing Saturday."

"Wow."

"Yeah," he said, his voice lowering. "She's been trying to get him to try prosthetics for like two years. I just hope this will help."

Class began, and I'll admit, I wasn't smiling right then because what Jaylen said kind of knocked the wind clean out of me.

Before lunch, Mr. Peters—the music guy— called me over to his room. He was one of the younger teachers, and he seemed pretty cool, but being how I wasn't in a music class I had no idea why he wanted to see me.

"Jackson, right?"

"Yeah," I said, looking around, forgetting about the smiling thing.

"I'm Mr. Peters, I teach music." He gestured toward his classroom. "I hear you play the drums?"

I nodded. "Uh huh."

"Great. So uh, we are getting the plans together for our big winter play and we're looking for a drummer. I had to fill in last year, and it was a little rough with me being a guitarist and all. You think you might be interested?"

I nodded without thinking. "Sure, I could do it."

"Great. I'll put you down. If you change your mind just let me know. Like I said, practice won't start until next month—just a few days a week after school. Thanks, Jackson."

"Sure."

Mr. Peters smiled and turned back for his classroom, which from where I stood looked pretty cool with all the music holders cluttered together and band instruments scattered on the shelf. I even spotted a Ray Charles poster squeezed in between the classical stuff.

I strode down the hall toward the cafeteria. Sitting down, Miranda shot me a look. "I'm impressed."

"What?"

"The smile, it's still there."

I told her about Mr. Peters and the play. She freaked. "See, all because you were smiling. You're approachable."

Jaylen and Megan laughed. But the truth was, my smile was real, but only for a moment, because two tables over sat the biggest jerk in the school.

I hadn't seen Brice since gym class yesterday, and just the sight of his face sent a wash of chill-tingling, smile-erasing emotions down my spine, which did not go unnoticed.

"Jack. Over here." Miranda waved her hands to get my attention. "Don't worry about him." I pulled my sandwich out of my bag—a smeared and soggy mystery.

"So, I heard there may be a few thousand people at this thing Saturday," Megan said, and soon everyone was talking about the band. As for my sandwich, I narrowed it down to either chicken or tuna salad.

Jaylen wiggled his fingers, playing the air bass. "Yeah well, they should prepare to be wowed."

I was hardly paying attention because Brice made a show of nodding my way and ducking his head to whisper. All heads at his table whipped around to get a better look at me.

I dropped my sandwich, which was definitely tuna. My face burned as anger coursed through my body. The murmur of conversations in the cafeteria, the rumors swirling with the steamed vegetables and macaroni and cheese. My jaw went tight, smile gone. Then I thought about Miranda, what Dad had said out on the rooftop. Arnie. When I opened my eyes, Miranda, Jaylen, and Megan were all staring at me.

"Hey guys, I'll be back." I slid out my chair and fixed a smile on my face. Miranda and Megan's eyes grew wide with panic. Jaylen grinned.

Miranda spoke first. "Jack. What are you doing?"

"No idea," I said, my smile locked down like a ventriloquist. I waved at Brice, starting for his table. The smug grin flew from his face as the lunch chatter went silent. More heads turned. I strutted right up to the "cool" table with a big old goofy smile. All eyes aimed at me. "What's up guys? How is everyone today?"

Everyone stopped what they were doing. Brice snorted and Danny gawked. I saw a few half smiles—well, not quite frowns, maybe. Some giggling, but I drowned it out with my smile and just continued yapping. "All right, sounds good. Hey look. So, the Wallywalkers are playing at the Fall Bash downtown this weekend, and we'd love to see you guys there, showing your support. Our charity is the Wounded Warriors, so come on. What do you say?"

Soon as I said it, something weird happened. Brice's eyes widened, and his smirk vanished. Only for a second, but enough that I dropped my smile, and for a blink we stood looking at each other without snarling. I shook it off quickly because we had an audience. "Well," I said, back on track. "I'll take that as a yes. Oh, and good luck this week against Jefferson. I hear they're really, *really* big."

I spun around and nearly collided into Mr. Sanchez, who was blocking my way and watching intently. My smile dropped but his didn't. He bowed his head and gestured toward my table. "That's the spirit, Mr. Dufresne."

CHAPTER 35

I waltzed into the kitchen where John Lee Hooker was rumbling through the surround sound. Vicki and Dad stood cutting vegetables on the counter.

"What's for dinner?" I asked, and Vicki turned around and smiled. She had a nice smile and one of those easy to like faces. Besides, it was kind of nice having company in the house.

"Eggplant Parmesan," Dad yelled over the music.

"Count me out."

"Oh come on, Jack, you know I can cook," Dad said, and I peeked over just as Vicki cut into what looked like a balloon.

"I really, uh, I don't know."

"Just like you didn't know about meatloaf, and I seem to remember serving seconds. Or was it thirds?" Dad had been trying all sorts of new recipes lately, and some of them had turned out not so bad.

I shrugged, pouring water into my faded New York Rangers cup. "I'll try it, but only because you have a guest."

"Such a charmer," Vicki said, winking at me.

"Yeah, when he wants to be," Dad groaned.

In the living room I found a box of t-shirts spilling onto the couch. I held up a black one, the word "Warriors" in yellow. "Cool."

"Oh yeah, so what do you think?" Dad said, peering in. "Vicki had those made up for us. Cool huh?"

I nodded, looking it over. "Jaylen's gonna flip."

I pulled a shirt over my head, breathing in the fumes of the fresh print. Vicki had basically become our publicist. She'd designed a really cool website where you could donate pledges online. And she'd agreed to help out at the volunteer tent with Mrs. Walker and Jaylen's mom. So yeah, Vicki wasn't all that bad.

Dinner was surprisingly good. Like spaghetti, I guess. After we ate, Dad read over the email from the Fall Bash people. "There are all sorts of causes, feeding the homeless, Breast Cancer, and The Humane Society, Diabetes and...oh, and how about this one?" He tapped the page. "Here's one for bugs' rights."

"No way!" I said, leaning over his shoulder.

"Yep, some band named *No Soap*. "It says here bugs have every right to the land."

"I consider myself a fairly liberal chick," Vicki said, sitting back on the couch, "but a girl needs her soap and bug spray."

THURSDAY'S MORNING announcements led with the big football game that afternoon. The Jefferson Tigers were coming, and the Claremont faithful needed to show their full support. I zoned out until the speaker crackled to life as Miranda's voice commanded the attention of the school.

"And also Rhinos, don't forget about the Fall Bash this Saturday down at the Riverfront," Miranda blared, half distorted because she was yelling into the microphone. An adjustment over the speaker, and I guessed Megan was telling her to take it down a notch. *"Oh, okay. And there will be candy corn, prizes, a pumpkin carving contest, and don't forget to come out and support our very own band, The Wallywalkers, who are taking pledges for The Wounded Warriors. See you there!"*

I continued with the smiling. In class, in the hallways. Not in the bathroom, because that would be weird. But I did get a few *See you Saturday's* in passing, so it was cool. Then something really strange happened.

I was running late for gym class after catching up again with Mr. Peters in the hallway. Turned out, he was playing banjo with The Blue Mountain Boys, a bluegrass band performing at the bash on Saturday. Kind of cool for a teacher. Anyway, I busted into the locker room to dress out as fast as I could, yanking on my laces when I heard footsteps.

I looked up, preparing to catch some flak from Mr. Hatch. Instead I locked eyes with my favorite jerk.

"Drummer Boy."

I got to my feet as he stepped into the rectangle of sunlight on the floor between us, wearing his usual Hollister t-shirt and fancy basketball shorts. Only his cocky grin was missing. He held his palms up and mumbled something like, "It's cool."

I stood there, my Plattsburgh State tee half tucked, my untied laces on the yellowed tile floor. A drippy faucet the only sound between us. Brice looked at my feet like he was thinking about what to say. I tried to think up something to say back to him when he shrugged. "Hey man, I just wanted to say it's cool you guys are doing the fund raiser this weekend."

I waited for the punchline, still skeptical, thinking the football team was about to rush in and laugh. After a quick sweep of the locker room I looked him in the eyes. "Yeah?"

His shoulders dropped and his eyes fell to the floor, then slowly back to me. "No, I'm for real. My uncle is in Afghanistan, he's supposed to be coming home next month." His gaze fell back to the floor in thought. "I uh, I just wanted to say I'll be there, with the rest of the school."

I never saw it coming. A whistle from the gym pierced the silence hanging in the room. Brice, the king, the villain, the jerk

I'd wanted to pummel, stuck out his hand as a peace offering. I took it and nodded. "Cool man, thanks."

His face showed relief, what looked to be a real smile. He started for the gym and then turned to me as I was tying up my shoes. "Dude, I can't believe you don't play football."

I shook my head with a laugh. Sure, we weren't going to be best friends or anything, and he still owed Miranda and Trevor each an apology, but maybe we could get to a truce or an understanding. Maybe there was hope for Brice Wilkes after all.

CHAPTER 36

On Saturday morning—the big day—I woke up to find a notebook beside my bed. I rubbed my eyes at the sight of Dad's journal, the one he kept by his nightstand. I flipped through the pages until I saw an entry dated yesterday.

Jackson,

I just wanted to let you see the newest entry in my diary. No more secrets, remember? Hey, maybe it means I can write to two people and stop boring your mother with all of the hockey talk. Ba dump bump.

Anyway, here goes the mushy part. Don't say I didn't warn you.

You're a great kid, Jack. Greater than anything your mother or I could have ever dreamed or hoped for. Well, I have a feeling she knew how great you'd be, but every day you find a way to amaze me. I don't know where I'd be without you.

As I'm sure you've gathered from reading these notebooks, I carry a lot of pain, pain I've carried quietly, tucked away in an effort to protect you. These journals have been my release, and I hope you understand some of this is just me letting go. But I miss her, Jack. I do. Every day I miss her so much.

I'm flawed, son. And for too long I've tried to hide my flaws from you, to appear happy and content so you would never worry about me or about us. I guess by doing that, I stole her away from you. I only hope you can forgive me.

She was amazing, Jack. Sure, she was flawed too. She was

only human, after all. But she was the kindest, most wonderful human being I've ever known, and she cared about you so much. She worried for you as only a mother can. You deserve to know her, Jack. I owe you that much. And I promise from this day forward to share her with you.

When I look out in the crowd tomorrow, maybe we'll see her. Because I know she'll be watching us. Somewhere, she'll be beaming with pride when she sees you. Just like I do every day.

Lastly, I want to thank you for sticking it out with me. You've handled this well, even as I've made some mistakes along the way. News flash, I'll probably make a few more. But I just hope you will trust that I love you more than anything in the world, Jack.

Love,

Dad

I read it twice before getting out of bed, then a third time before I skipped down the stairs and found the big lug in the kitchen. Without a word I launched into him for a hug. He grunted, patted my head, and that's about all you need to know about our little moment.

Dad served up bacon and eggs. He'd just gotten off the phone with Vicki. We'd already raised close to three hundred bucks for the Wounded Warriors Foundation. The volunteers were thrilled with our impressive start. Depending on the turnout today, a thousand bucks wasn't out of reach.

Things got rolling. Our phones buzzed and dinged and we were on the move. Outside it was cool and cloudy. Dad said the temperatures were supposed to heat up, approaching sixty degrees by noon. I could get used to this fall thing.

I loaded my drums into the Walkers' van. We packed the rest of the equipment into Dad's trunk, and more still into

Vicki's Subaru and Mr. Carter's Windstar. As our caravan made the turnaround at the end of our street, we honked and cheered like crazy. The Wallywalkers were headed downtown.

The clouds were breaking by the time we arrived at the amphitheater where we unloaded our equipment. The grass glistened as vending tents lined the field, setting up to sell everything from homemade crafts and jewelry to soaps and even homemade dog treats— we snagged a few breath mints for Wally.

The smokers and grills pumped out a savory plume over the grounds. Miranda and I escaped for a quick walk down by the river. She wore a plaid button down, jeans, and her usual canvas shoes. Nothing crazy, but when I looked into her eyes...

Miranda always griped about how her parents never let her wear makeup. But for the show they'd relented, and Megan had brushed her eyelids with bright blue sparkly eye shadow. Her hair was out, hardly tamed by two shiny clips on the sides and the result was stunning. We all knew she had the singing thing down, but now she looked the part.

"So was it right *here* where you smacked Brice?" I asked, hopping to a spot every few feet. I'd told her about Brice in the locker room and she'd flipped. But now she was so quiet, and I was getting worried.

"Come on, don't tell me you're nervous?"

She grinned. "A little. I'll be all right once I get up there."

"Maybe Trevor can find another pair of sunglasses. I think I saw some—"

"Jack." She laughed.

"Yeah?"

She took my hand and we stopped. I stared into her golden eyes. Her voice was lower, serious. "It's just...well, I'm really glad you moved down here."

"Oh. Well, I never thought I'd say this, but I am too."

She closed her eyes, flashing a wash of sparkly blue with her smile. "But uh, I mean. I don't know how to ask this, but um, are we like... you know?" I wasn't sure what she was asking. I'd never seen Miranda so timid. I was about to ask what she was talking about when she rolled her eyes and laughed.

And then I got it. I jumped, causing her to jump too. "Oh! Yes! I mean, of course. Yeah."

Miranda gushed, unleashing her stare-worthy smile. I nodded, taking her hand as we started walking again in silence, officially a couple and with big goofy grins on our faces. The day was already a winner as far as I was concerned. Across the field on the stage, the first band was ready to kick things off.

With a name like Mud Bucket, I expected something heavy, but heavy didn't cut it. Imagine a chainsaw cutting through a rusty barrel as someone screamed over the noise. Not even close. If anyone was still sleepy when they arrived at the fifteenth annual Fall Bash Fund Drive, they were soon wide awake as the opening act slammed into their set.

I stepped back, absorbing the force of their sound. Those guys grinded, like a train slamming into the audience, the lead singer throttled the bleary crowd with wails of agony. Jaylen's jaw hit his chest. Trevor actually covered his ears until Mr. Walker shook his head. It wasn't even noon yet and these guys were full blast. I only hoped they were raising money for the deaf, because my ears would never be the same.

After the first song, Mr. Walker said something to Dad and we all trooped toward the barbeque trucks, the farthest point from the stage we could find without leaving, but not nearly far enough. A rocket launch was more delicate than Mud Bucket.

The next band was a welcome relief, a soft, acoustic whispering band that healed our ears after the metal-wrenching we'd just experienced. We clapped along as the two barefoot girls strummed and swayed in the sunshine like angels of mercy.

Trevor whipped out his shades and deftly placed them over his eyes. "So, what do you think?"

"That's the coolest trumpet player I've ever seen," Jaylen said, pulling out his own shades. Dad did the same.

"Oh wow," Miranda laughed. "I think we are easily the coolest *band* here."

"So we have our songs?" Dad asked, even though he knew we did.

"Dad, are we doing your song?" I asked. He looked around, fidgeting. Great. The last thing we needed was for our lead guitarist to get the jitters.

"I don't know, I think we should stick to the covers."

"Well, we kind of need to figure it out," I said through a mouthful of pork. This southern thing was growing on me.

"Let's start with the fun stuff and see how it goes," he said. I looked to Miranda, my *girlfriend*. Something told me we were playing Dad's song, whether he knew it or not.

Mr. Carter wiped his mouth, clearing his throat as he rolled his chair closer to the table. His face was tight and serious. He had our full attention as he allowed Mrs. Carter to edge him closer. She put a hand on his. He took a sip of his water and nodded. A round of applause drifted over the gathering crowd as the girls on stage took a bow.

"Hey so, I wanted to say thanks to you all." He took a breath, shut his eyes, and his mouth went tight. "It means a lot to me, more than you know, all the support and everything you're doing."

Jaylen set his hand on his dad's arm. Mr. Carter turned to his son, his eyes moist and full of love. "I'm so proud of you, Jaylen."

We all nodded silently. Miranda dabbed at her eyes. Bad day for makeup.

"Thank you, Alan," Dad said quietly. Another band was

setting up on the stage and the amps screeched with feedback. Mr. Carter looked up with a smile.

"All right, enough of that. Now go break a leg!"

Everyone stared at him. He rolled his head back towards Mrs. Carter. "My first joke and it bombs. Lighten up guys, come on."

With two bands to go before we went on, my own pre-show jitters arrived. My hands tingled and my feet started sweating. There must have been a thousand people walking around and more kept coming through the gates. The tents were busy. It was pretty cool, all of the causes, the clipboards filled with forms as people signed up for walks, 5k's, bowling, raffle tickets. Even a dog show. But that didn't help my nerves.

I recognized some faces in the crowd. In fact, it seemed like all of Claremont Middle was there. Mr. Peters found me at our tent. I almost didn't recognize him, wearing a straw hat, long sleeve t-shirt, and faded shorts. "Hey Jack. You guys getting ready to go on?"

I nodded. "Yeah."

"Well, good luck. We're not playing until four."

"Yeah, I don't know." I looked out to the massive swell of people on the field.

"Hey, don't be nervous. We're just here to have a good time and raise some money." He arched an eyebrow. "Besides, word has it Miranda can really sing."

You just wait, I thought. "Yeah, she can, but I think everyone's deaf after Mud Bucket."

His eyes widened with his smile. "Oh, you're not kidding. Yikes."

"So, what's your charity?" I asked, glancing over his shoulder at the tents.

"Autism Awareness."

"Cool, good luck to you guys. See ya, Mr. Peters."

Onstage, the Free Loaders were fumbling through a pretty awful cover of Boston's "More Than a Feeling" when we met up backstage. Dad spoke to an organizer, who pointed up to the stage with a hand held radio. Miranda snapped her fingers and paced the lawn, singing to herself. I tapped my sticks. Trevor was Trevor. And then there was Jaylen, all smiles and on a mission for his dad.

I sat down beside him at a picnic table. "Man, one more song and then we're on."

"Yep."

"You're not even a little nervous?" I asked. He looked so calm. Like he could take a nap.

"Maybe a little." He shrugged.

"I wasn't...didn't think I was. But there's a lot of people out there."

Jaylen turned to me, his eyes squinting in the midday sun. "Just think of it like the high dive at the pool. Were you scared then?"

"Dude, yeah. I was terrified."

"But you still jumped off like it was nothing. So, what's a few people? We got this, man." He pushed me playfully and I laughed. The crowd cheered as The Free Loaders took a bow. I stretched my lungs with a deep breath. We were up.

Adjusting my drums, the butterflies fought for space in my ribcage. The sound of the crowd rushed over me, the pockets of conversations buzzing as they waited for us—like a wave of faces and voices and smells ripping toward us, ready to crash down and topple us. I tightened my cymbals and glanced over to Dad. He adjusted his strings. When he looked up and smiled I saw a bit of Grandpa's twinkle in his eyes.

The emcee came out and made the introductions. I rocked in place on my stool. This was it.

"All right, Miranda, take us away," Dad said, strapping on

the guitar. She turned around and gave me a wink. She was fine. We were fine. I focused on the scuff marks on my snare drum. We were back in the basement just having a good time. I nodded to Jaylen, who bobbed his head. Trevor took a spritz of his inhaler and then gripped his horn. Dad counted us down.

"One... Two... Three..."

And we were off. Jaylen strutted and Trevor puffed his cheeks into his trumpet. We rolled into *I Feel Good* and Miranda let it go like I'd never heard before. Even Dad whirled his head around as she took the mic and did her thing. Fingers pointed, heads swiveled, jaws dropped. You know, the usual.

So Good... So Good... I got you... Owwww!

When Miranda said "Owww" and started dancing, the crowd lost its mind. She shuffled her feet, slid one way then back. We fed off her energy. She was a blur of rhythm and tapping. She skipped back to the microphone and dipped her head back, her shoulders shimmying to the beat. Man was she on.

At some point my arms took over, everything became involuntary. I laughed as phones and cameras went up, and the crowd swept into a collective frenzy. By the time we finished our first song, the big, cresting wave had crashed. Only we were the wave and no one knew what hit them. They yelled and whistled, clapping and chanting for more.

My chest heaved but it was a good kind of energy. Miranda wiped her forehead. She turned back to me, eyes wide, holding the sides of her face with her hands and mouthed, "Wow!"

Dad leaned over to Jaylen and Jaylen to Miranda, then yelled back to me "Respect." I came in with the beat and Trevor plowed ahead on the horn. Mr. Carter had said Miranda had to do an Aretha Franklin song, and he was right. I liked it because we did a fast version, and I got to bang away. We were full speed ahead and playing with nervous energy, but the crowd was on our side. Miranda had ignited us.

At the bridge, Miranda strutted back and forth on the stage, her confidence surging, wagging her finger and commanding her audience. We brought it down low and Miranda did her best Aretha impression, ad-libbing and interacting with the crowd before we came back with the chorus. If you've ever seen footage of a star before they were famous, that was exactly what it was, watching Miranda do her thing. Her voice was a net, cast out to sea by the speakers to capture the crowd and drag them in.

She was a star, and I had the best seat in the house.

After "Respect," even the band setting up behind the stage abandoned what they were doing and stood behind us, clapping and cheering us on. A scraggily guy covered with tattoos whistled and yelled to me that Miranda needed to be on *America's Got Talent*. I nodded, twirled my sticks. Out in the crowd, heads shook in awe, spelled by Miranda's magic.

With one song left, Dad had become preoccupied with the guitar pedal at his feet. Miranda said something to him, and he nodded. She placed the microphone back on the stand and looked out to the adoring crowd.

"This last song is an original."

My heart flailed. This was it. We were really doing Dad's song. Mom's song. Our song.

Jaylen smiled. We were all sweating and heaving. I gripped my drumsticks and Miranda peeked back at me with a blinding white smile. The buzz from "Respect" faded. We all waited for Dad. It seemed like forever, the five of us there on stage, taking it in. The crowd was hungry and murmuring. Finally, Miranda stepped closer to the microphone and began singing Dad's song without us. Just a girl and her voice and the words to my mother.

> *I feel your warmth in the sun*
> *Hear your whisper in the wind*
> *Each wave is a kiss*

Miranda turned to Dad and his hands found the guitar, strumming the opening chords, Jaylen followed and I tapped the rim of the drum. The song took flight, slow down the runway, picking up speed. Then Miranda took it away.

> *You'd want me to carry on*
> *But I don't know where to begin*
> *It's these moments I'll miss*

The crowd roared with approval, and to anyone watching, Dad might've looked a world away in thought. But I knew exactly where he was.

Afterwards Miranda took a bow to the chants and whistles. I scanned the field, a choppy sea of faces and colors. Dad called me up, and I joined Trevor and Jaylen for a bow. The Wallywalkers. How did this happen? If someone had told me three months ago, I would have never believed it.

Off stage we were greeted by the Walkers, the Carters, and Vicki. Everyone grabbed and hugged us with congratulations.

"That was amazing!" Vicki said, dabbing her eyes. Dad smiled and shot me a wink.

We were mobbed by our newfound fans from school. Miranda was a celebrity, and I not so teasingly asked her if she needed a pen to sign autographs.

We spent the rest of the afternoon basking in the sun, watching the show. Trevor rolled his eyes when he saw Miranda and I holding hands and said he knew it all along. We laughed as every few steps we were stopped and congratulated. A guy from *The Times* took a group picture and, judging by the kids from school, we were going to need a bigger lunch table.

And it wasn't just the kids. We even had an offer to open up for *The Soul Blasters*, the headliners who'd already raised over two-thousand-dollars for the local Daily Bread chapter. Dad said maybe, but we all knew he wasn't taking us out on the road. Anyway, our donations were up to $952 and still coming in. Not too shabby for some kids. Vicki said our donations spiked during our set, with people talking about the girl with the voice.

You know, my girlfriend.

We loaded up the car while Vicki helped take down the tent. She promised to meet us back at the house with everyone else for a celebration. Riding home with Dad, the temperatures had dropped with the clouds, and when I reached over and turned the thermostat to warm, Dad turned to me with a grin.

"Don't tell me you're cold?"

"Just a little."

"The next thing I know you'll be drinking sweet tea and saying ya'll."

I shrugged. "It's not so bad."

"So you admit it? That you're starting to like it down here?"

"It has its moments."

"Like today?"

I nodded, rubbing my arms. Maybe it *was* time to break out the jackets.

"I think your mom would have been proud of you today," Dad said.

I smiled. "You mean proud of *us*."

"Yeah, proud of us."

We drove in silence for a moment, and I thought about my mom's face. I turned to Dad. "Did you see her out in the crowd, watching us?"

"I think so. It sure felt like she was there."

"Yeah."

Dad nodded, his face looking straight away, somewhere between a memory and a smile. I sat back in my seat, knowing I had everything I could ask for in a dad. And now I sort of had my mom, too. It was like her memory had moved down here with us. It was inside of me, in my laughter and my thoughts. It was crazy, because home wasn't up North or down South.

It was right here, in these moments with my dad.

ACKNOWLEDGMENTS

While this story is fictional, Jack's dad was based on someone I know very well. Growing up, my dad was the strongest, smartest, funniest person I knew. He was like my own personal super hero. On his way to work one morning, his car was hit by a train. The train smashed into the driver's side door, flipped the car over then hit it again to sweep it from the tracks. Miraculously, my dad walked away with a scratch on his arm. *See?* I remember thinking to myself. *Superman.*

We played football in the living room. My dad would get on his knees and I'd try to leap over him to score a touchdown. I'd beg to do it again and again and again, until we broke something or one of us got hurt. Those were the days.

It wasn't until I had a kid of my own that I realized my father wasn't a superhero. He was human, with human worries and doubts. He'd hurt his back when he was younger and it would flare up from time to time. He went to work every day at four in the morning. And yet, there was always time for those football games, to hoist me up over his shoulders, to become the model of everything I want to be for my own kids.

So thanks, Dad, for everything. For backyard football, minibikes, flea markets, and Saturday mornings together. For long drives, action movies and hot air balloon rides and bb guns. For those goal line stands in the living room. Most of all, thanks for always having time.

This book took the long road to publication. As usual, there are so many people who pitched in along the way, starting with my wife, Anne, for helping me with all things Plattsburgh. To my North Country family, John and Jocelyne Lavigne. To

Diane Fanning for the early reads. To Staci Olsen for liking my story. To Holli Anderson for all the fine tuning. To Nana, for a lifetime of encouragement. To Simon, for taking on the high dive (you're ten, right?). To Bella, who looks at me like she believes I can do anything, even when my back hurts or I'm tired.

ABOUT THE AUTHOR

Pete Fanning is the author of *Justice in a Bottle* and *Runaway Blues*. He lives in Virginia with his wife, son, baby girl, and two very spoiled dogs. He can be found at www.petefanning.com, where he's posted over 200 flash fiction stories.

This has been an
Immortal Production

www.ingramcontent.com/pod-product-compliance
Lightning Source LLC
Chambersburg PA
CBHW030621190726
48286CB00008B/2351